© Kathrin Brussig

THOMAS BRUSSIG

The Short End of the Sonnenallee

TRANSLATED BY JONATHAN FRANZEN AND JENNY WATSON

Thomas Brussig is the author of seven novels, including *Wie es leuchtet* and *Helden wie wir* (*Heroes Like Us*, FSG, 1997). As a screenwriter, he worked with Edgar Reitz on his *Heimat* epic. Born in East Berlin, Brussig now divides his time between Berlin and Mecklenburg.

Jonathan Franzen is the author of six novels, including *The Corrections*, *Freedom*, *Purity*, and *Crossroads*, and five works of nonfiction, most recently *The Kraus Project* and *The End of the End of the Earth*, all published by Farrar, Straus and Giroux.

Jenny Watson is an associate professor of German at Marquette University. Since receiving her PhD in German and Scandinavian literature, Watson has published many books and articles, including *German Milwaukee*, "Selma Lagerlöf: Surface and Depth," and *Scandinavia and Germany: Cross-Cultural Currents*. She lives in Milwaukee, Wisconsin.

ALSO BY THOMAS BRUSSIG

Heroes Like Us

The Short End of the Sonnenallee

The Short End of the Sonnenallee

Thomas Brussig

TRANSLATED FROM THE GERMAN BY
JONATHAN FRANZEN AND JENNY WATSON

INTRODUCTION BY JONATHAN FRANZEN

PICADOR ▪ New York

Picador
120 Broadway, New York 10271

Library of Congress Cataloging-in-Publication Data
Names: Brussig, Thomas, 1964– author. | Franzen, Jonathan, translator. |
    Watson, Jenny (Translator), translator.
Title: The short end of the Sonnenallee / Thomas Brussig ; translated
    from the German by Jonathan Franzen and Jenny Watson; introduction
    by Jonathan Franzen.
Other titles: Am kürzeren Ende der Sonnenallee. English
Description: First American edition. | New York : Picador, 2023.
Identifiers: LCCN 2022057944 | ISBN 9781250878991 (paperback)
Subjects: LCGFT: Satirical literature. | Novels.
Classification: LCC PT2662.R87 A413 2023 | DDC 833/.92—
    dc23/eng/20221205
LC record available at https://lccn.loc.gov/2022057944

Designed by Gretchen Achilles

Our books may be purchased in bulk for promotional, educational,
or business use. Please contact your local bookseller or the Macmillan
Corporate and Premium Sales Department at 1-800-221-7945, extension
5442, or by email at MacmillanSpecialMarkets@macmillan.com.

For book club information, please visit facebook.com/picadorbookclub
or email marketing@picadorusa.com.

picadorusa.com • instagram.com/picador
twitter.com/picadorusa • facebook.com/picadorusa

10 9 8 7 6 5 4 3 2 1

For my parents, Sigune and Siegfried Brussig

Introduction

by Jonathan Franzen

It's fitting that *The Short End of the Sonnenallee* ends with the appearance of a man who literally works miracles, because the novel itself is a kind of miracle. Set in the last decade of the German Democratic Republic, thirty-odd years into the East German experiment in totalitarian surveillance and rigid ideological conformity, and written in hindsight, ten years after the fall of the Berlin Wall and the reunification of Germany, the novel should by all rights be a reckoning with the tragedy of that experiment—with its terrors and injustices, its mendacity and bleakness. A firm rule of the literature of Eastern Europe under communism, whether the philosophical ironies of Milan Kundera, the coded fables of Ismail Kadare, or the metaphysical theatrics of Václav Havel, is that its intentions be *serious*. And no Soviet-satellite European state was more serious than East Germany. The country was essentially a giant prison, its western borders heavily fortified and lined with a "death strip," on which citizens trying to flee across it would be shot, and the world had never witnessed a system of political surveillance more pervasive than the one developed by the Stasi, the GDR's state security service, which maintained files on more than one-third of the country's population. After the Wall came down, in 1989, two basic emotional positions were available to survivors of the regime. You could be angry about the decades of privation and repression, the betrayals by your neighbors, the lies in which you'd been forced to participate, the corruption and hypocrisy of the Party leadership. Alternatively, if you were a worker who'd had a decent life under the regime, you might feel regret for the passing of the proletarian dictatorship, resentment of the crass materialism and economic insecurities that the conquering West brought with it. Either way, looking back, you were serious. And this is the miracle of Thomas Brussig. When he looks back, in *The Short End of the Sonnenallee*, he does it without anger or regret. What he sees is neither a dystopia nor a utopia but something poignant. He sees people being people, the way people have always been and always will be. He also, miraculously, sees something silly.

It helps, in this regard, that the novel's main characters are adolescent boys: the desires and troubles of teenagers are seldom far from silliness. The novel's brilliant stroke is to highlight their silliness by situating it in the most serious of places. Their families all live up against the Wall, on the runt end of a street, the Sonnenallee, that protrudes from West Berlin into the Soviet Zone. Their windows look out on the death strip, on towers where soldiers stand waiting to shoot would-be escapees, and on a barricaded checkpoint for traffic from the West. Directly beyond the Wall is an observation platform from which curious Westerners can gawk at the death strip. The boys of the Sonnenallee are so tantalizingly close to freedom that they can hear the gawkers and shout back to them, even as the West remains as inaccessible to them as the moon. An ordinary novel might play up the sorrow of their situation. An extraordinary novel, while acknowledging the sorrow, plays up its ridiculousness.

The border, though closed to the teenage characters, is not so impermeable that they're not all mad for the West. They have access to Western television, they have Western relatives (and know smugglers) who can get them Western goods, and the girl they're all in love with, the great beauty of the Sonnenallee, Miriam, is obsessed with making out with Western boys, who are free to cross the border. Most important, they have politically forbidden music, which they record on their tape recorders from Western radio shows of the era, such as *SFBeat*. They may have grown up under a regime whose repressive ambitions rival North Korea's, and they may be continually deprived, but the texture of their daily lives is paradoxically one of fullness. In their scavenging and resourceful way, they experience the West more vividly, and appreciate it more deeply, than Westerners themselves do. Characteristic of Brussig's humane vision—his charting of a middle way between denunciation of the East for its political excesses and resentment of the West for its material excesses—is his rendering of deprivation as a kind of blessing. In the words of one of the novel's more thoughtful young characters, Mario, "Wanting something is much more interesting than having it."

To be sure, the socialist state is always there, and Brussig gives the evils and annoyances of totalitarianism their due.

The younger characters live in fear of ruining their life prospects through some minor offense against the state (or, almost as bad, of being compelled to give a self-critical presentation at school), while the older characters fear the Stasi and the Russians. No one who's not connected with the Stasi can get a telephone at home, and no one but the very privileged can get a car repaired in less than a month. Apartments are cramped, running water is intermittent, store lines are long, travel in the East is restricted, travel to the West forbidden altogether, and elections are a travesty: every adult citizen is expected to cast a vote for the only slate of candidates on the ballot. Young people display their patriotism, willingly or not, by joining the official socialist youth group, the Free German Youth, and marching in parades on Republic Day, the Seventh of October.

In a world of scarcity and distrust, in which absolutely everything is political, the one thing the people of the Sonnenallee can count on is each other. The remarkable ease and closeness of their friendships is central to the novel's charm. (I'm hard pressed to think of a novel in which people treat their neighbors with more consistent kindness.) Figures who first appear in the book as menacing or upsetting outsiders— the local beat cop, who bears the maladroit East German title of Designated Precinct Enforcer; the checkpoint border guard, who's fervently convinced of communism's eventual global triumph; the two gay assistants at the local dance school, who are dubbed, with the casual homophobia of high school boys, the Dancing Pansies—become magically humanized as they're drawn into the Sonnenallee community. Even plainly odious minor characters, such as a fanatically disciplinarian army commandant, or a Party functionary whose job is to police counterrevolutionary thought, acquire unexpected poignancy as they fall victim to the absurdities of the East German state. Only from irredeemably dogmatic characters does Brussig withhold his sympathy. And, even there, the narrative moves in such a way as simply to exclude them from the circle of sympathy and leave them to their own devices, as if to be denied access to a community of kindness is punishment enough.

Is the warmth in Brussig's depiction of the GDR realistic? Not having lived there, I'm in no position to judge, but I would guess that the answer is yes and no. The uses of adversity are famously sweet, and it makes sense that friendship and its paired foundations, trust and love, would be all the more precious, all the more intensely felt, in a society determined to erode them in service to political obedience. But a novel is an invented thing, its content a selected thing, and I can't help thinking that what's ultimately being depicted is not a society but one very unusual person's relationship to it. The East German writer who can portray a community so lovably and laughably is a writer whose sense of humor and capacity for forgiveness survived totalitarianism miraculously intact. Although the details of life in the GDR are realistic, the story to which they're harnessed has the inwardness and self-sufficiency of something deeply personal. The events in the book are a bit too funny to be true to life, its plot turns a bit too neat. Again and again, Brussig introduces odd little circumstances and incidental story lines that seem to go nowhere, only to pick them up later and resolve them into perfect narrative punch lines. By the end of the book, when the last of the jokes has paid off, it's clear that, although we've recognizably been in communist East Berlin, we've been no less inside the heart of Thomas Brussig. The very title of the book is a declaration of his independence. Defying the one adjective we all associate with life behind the Iron Curtain, the word *dark*, Brussig gives us the word *Sonnenallee*—Boulevard of the Sun. The street name is real and can be found on a map, and where a different writer might have used its warmth and its poetry to telegraph irony, Brussig deploys it as a straightforward correction of our assumptions about life in the East. When Berlin was partitioned, in 1945, the Allies claimed almost the entire length of the Sonnenallee. But East Berlin, too, got its piece of the sun.

If the short end of the Sonnenallee is a charmed space, a place where silliness and true love are possible, the contours of this space are those of recollection in tranquility. Not only is the novel's chronology nonlinear, it can't even really be sorted out. The storytelling moves in the disordered way that memory itself does. One scene leads to another by free association; incidents are grouped more by theme than by sequence. *These are all the things that happened,* the narrator seems to say, *but I'll be damned if I can remember which thing followed which.* The effect is to heighten the sense of enchantment, the fairy-tale feeling of "Once upon a time," the mood of a dream in which motifs keep recurring. But Brussig's method is also *more* realistic than a conventional telling would be, because we don't remember our lives the way a novel typically organizes lives. Although *The Short End of the Sonnenallee* is refreshingly unserious in tone and content, its form reflects a deeper kind of seriousness. When a state has collapsed and vanished, when a crushingly thorough political experiment has failed, all that remains is memory. What matters afterward is less the GDR itself than how those who experienced it recall their lives in it: how they *choose* to recall them.

To laugh at the recollection of a dark time—specifically, a time in which the collective was paramount, the individual a nullity—is to reframe the notion of seriousness. The central image of *Sonnenallee* is that of an unread love letter that the novel's main character, Michael Kuppisch, ardently hopes (but can't be sure) is addressed to him, and that is carried out of his hands by the wind, up over the Wall outside his apartment building, and down onto the death strip. The Wall is the product of vast geopolitical and ideological forces: the devastation of Europe by the Nazis, the Cold War maneuverings of America and the Soviet Union, the logic of scientific socialism. While historians of the era rightly focus on these forces, the novelist focuses on a single sheet of paper, and on Michael Kuppisch's ridiculous attempts to retrieve it from the death strip, as if the truly serious struggle were not between East and West, not between competing ideologies, but between individual humanity and the weight of history.

Although this weight was especially heavy in East Berlin in the 1980s, Brussig's novel is relevant to our own times as well. The GDR may have been singularly rigorous in its intolerance of dissent, its demonization of its adversaries, its designation of certain words as taboo, and its creation of an atmosphere of paranoia, but Brussig's depiction of it in *Sonnenallee* is an unsettling premonition of our own political excesses, on both the left and the right, and of the anxieties of technology run amok. However much the Stasi knew about its subjects, Google and Facebook know far more about theirs. Now, as then, there are dogmas that must be publicly subscribed to, politically forbidden language to be avoided, for fear of having one's life ruined, and the very same kind of lies are propagated: Donald Trump was reelected by a landslide (if not quite with the 99 percent support achieved by the communist National Front), blue-state American cities are as ravaged by "criminality" as East German students were taught to believe the West was, and "enemies" both within and beyond our borders are bent on destroying our way of life. But *The Short End of the Sonnenallee* also stands as a reminder that, even when the public realm becomes a nightmare, people can still privately manage to preserve their humanity, and be silly, and forgive. If Brussig could do it in East Germany, of all places, anyone can do it anywhere.

* * *

I first read *The Short End of the Sonnenallee* at the urging of my friend Anne Rubesame, a native East Berliner, who was helping me with the GDR chapters of my novel *Purity*. "If you want to know what it was really like for us back then," she told me, "you've got to read Brussig." I proceeded to read Brussig and to borrow liberally, in *Purity*, from the spirit of *Sonnenallee* and his first novel, *Heroes Like Us*. I was surprised to discover that, although the latter had been translated into English, the former had not. *Sonnenallee* is the rare novel that not only made me laugh (again and again) but brought tears to my eyes (at the moment when it comes home to one of the older characters that she can never, ever be a Westerner). I couldn't believe that a novel so smart and so funny, so winningly readable, so original in its method, so relevant in its themes, hadn't found a wider international audience. I thought that someday I ought to try translating it myself.

For several years, the German edition sat on a shelf near my desk and quietly reproached me. Then, out of the blue, I got an email from a professor of German history and literature, Jenny Watson, who was frustrated that she couldn't teach *Sonnenallee* to her non-German-reading students at Marquette University. I told her that I shared her frustration, and I suggested that she translate the book herself. In remarkably short order, she sent me an energetic rough draft, which inspired me to finally undertake my own translation of Brussig's language. The resulting text is a dual labor of love, Jenny's and mine. I'm hugely grateful to her, for supplying the impetus and the groundwork for this edition; to Anne Rubesame, for reading the text and offering extremely helpful comments; and to Thomas Brussig himself, for unpacking the book's trickiest sentences and word choices and sharing his own thoughts about his accomplishment.

The Short End of
the Sonnenallee

Churchill's cold stub

Life abounds with opportunities to divulge your home address, and Michael Kuppisch had found that whenever he mentioned the Sonnenallee, the street where he lived in Berlin, people responded warmly, even sentimentally. In Michael Kuppisch's experience, the Sonnenallee was especially effective in moments of uncertainty or situations of outright tension. Even hostile Saxons almost always turned friendly when they learned they were dealing with a Berliner who lived on the Sonnenallee. Michael Kuppisch could well imagine that when Joseph Stalin, Harry S. Truman, and Winston Churchill were partitioning Berlin into zones, at the Potsdam Conference in the summer of 1945, the Sonnenallee had had something of the same effect. Especially on Stalin; dictators and despots have a well-known weakness for the whisperings of poetry. Stalin didn't want the Americans to get a street as beautifully named as the Sonnenallee, at least not all of it. He lodged a claim for the Sonnenallee with Harry S. Truman—which the latter naturally rejected. Stalin, however, refused to back down, and things quickly approached the point of blows. As Stalin and Truman squared off, nose to nose, the British premier squeezed in between them, separating them, and stepped over to the map of Berlin. He saw right away that the Sonnenallee was more than four kilometers long. Churchill was allied with the Americans by tradition, and everyone in the room assumed he would deny Stalin the Sonnenallee. Knowing Churchill, they expected him to take a puff of his cigar, ponder for a moment, then release the smoke, shake his head, and move on to the next point of negotiation. But when Churchill sucked on the stub, he was dismayed to find it cold. Stalin was kind enough to give him a light, and as Churchill savored his first puff and leaned over the map of Berlin, he wondered how he could adequately repay Stalin's kindness. Releasing the smoke, he gave Stalin a sixty-meter smidgen of the Sonnenallee and changed the subject.

That's how it must have gone, thought Michael Kuppisch. How else could such a long street have been divided so close to where it ended? Sometimes he also thought: If stupid Churchill had only paid attention to his cigar, we'd be living in the West now.

Michael Kuppisch was always looking for explanations because he was all too often confronted with things that didn't seem normal to him. It never ceased to amaze him that he lived on a street where the lowest house number was 379. He was likewise unable to ignore the *daily humiliation* of stepping out of his apartment building and being greeted with ridicule from the observation platform on the West side—entire school classes shouting and whistling and yelling, "Look, a real Zonie!" or "Zonie, come on, give us a little wave, we wanna take your picture!" And yet, strange as this all was, it was nothing compared to the utterly unbelievable sight of his first-ever love letter being carried by the wind into the death strip and coming to rest there—before he'd even read it.

Michael Kuppisch, whom everyone called Micha (except for his mother, who'd suddenly taken to calling him Misha), not only had a theory about why there was a short end of the Sonnenallee, he also had a theory about why *his* years at the short end of the Sonnenallee were the most interesting time there had ever been or ever would be. The only dwellings at the short end of the Sonnenallee were the legendary Q3A buildings, with their tiny cramped apartments. The only people willing to move into them were newlyweds whose one burning wish was to finally live together under one roof. But soon these newlyweds had children, which made the cramped apartments even more cramped. Moving into a bigger apartment was out of the question; the authorities counted the number of rooms, not square meters, and considered the families "provided for." Fortunately, this was happening in almost every household, and when Micha began to widen his life onto the streets, because he couldn't stand the cramped apartment anymore, he met a lot of other kids who felt more or less the same way. And because the same sort of thing was happening almost everywhere at the short end of the Sonnenallee, Micha felt part of a "potential." When his friends declared, "We're a clique," Micha said, "We're a potential." Even he didn't quite know what he was trying to say, but he felt it had to mean *something* that everyone came from the same cramped Q3A apartments and got together every day, wearing the same kind of clothes, listening to the same music, experiencing the same yearning, and feeling ever more strongly, with each passing day, that when they finally reached adulthood they would do everything, everything differently. Micha even considered it a promising sign that they all loved the same girl.

The condemned

They always met up at an abandoned playground—they themselves had been the kids who were supposed to play on this playground, but there hadn't been any more kids after them. Because no fifteen-year-old can say he's going to the playground, they called it "hanging out at the grounds," which sounded much more subversive. Then they listened to music, ideally illegal music. It was usually Micha who brought the new songs—no sooner had he recorded them from *SFBeat* than he'd play them at the grounds, even though they were too new to be illegal yet. A song's value skyrocketed when it was known to be illegal. "Hiroshima" was illegal, likewise "Je t'aime" and the Rolling Stones, who were banned from top to bottom. The most illegal song of all was "Moscow," by Wonderland. No one knew who banned the songs, still less the reason why.

"Moscow" had to be experienced in a kind of autistic blues ecstasy—with swaying movements and narrowed eyes, teeth

THOMAS BRUSSIG

buried in lower lips. It was all about exploring the consummate *blues feeling* and not hiding how deeply you were into it. There was nothing but the music and your swaying, and so they didn't notice, until it was far too late, that the Designated Precinct Enforcer had materialized at the very moment when Micha's friend Mario was crying out, in his fervor, "Oh, man, is this illegal! Totally illegal!" The DPE turned off the tape player and gloatingly asked, "What is illegal?"

Mario played innocent. "Illegal? What do you mean, illegal? Did someone here say illegal?" He quickly realized this wasn't going to work.

"Oh, you mean *illegal*," Micha said, as though relieved. "That's just young-person slang."

"The expression *illegal* is employed in teenage speech when the underage speaker wishes to express his enthusiasm," said Lensy, who read so much that he not only needed thick lenses but could effortlessly speak in arrogantly long sentences. "*Illegal* is, thus, a word that expresses approval."

"Like *dope* or *the bomb*," said Frizz, so named because he had hair like Jimi Hendrix.

"Other popular teenage slang expressions include *sick* or *killer*," said Lensy.

"But they all mean the same thing as *bad* or *insane* or, like we said, *illegal*," Fatty explained. Everyone was nodding fiercely, waiting to see what the DPE would say.

"Boys," he said, "do you take me for a fool? What *I* think you were discussing is how totally illegal it is to find a West German citizen's lost passport and not turn it in."

"No," said Micha. "Which is to say—yes, of course, we

know it's totally illegal, if you find a passport, not to turn it in. But that's not what we were talking about, Sergeant Horkefeld."

"*First* Sergeant," the DPE informed them severely. "I'm not a sergeant, I'm a first sergeant. It's a subleader rank. First you're sergeant, then staff sergeant, second sergeant, and first sergeant. But next week they're promoting me to sublieutenant. It's a commissioned rank."

"That is so interesting. Congratulations!" said Micha, happy that the patrolman had forgotten what he was actually at the grounds for. Instead of pursuing *illegality*, he was reciting service ranks.

"After sublieutenant comes second lieutenant, first lieutenant, captain, major, colonel—all gradations of officer."

Micha planted an elbow in the side of Lensy, who was choosing this of all moments, when the DPE's mood was improving, to take a deep breath and correct him on his usage of *gradations*.

"Then the general ranks: brigadier general, major general, lieutenant general, army general—you boys notice anything there?"

"There's a whole lot of ranks," said Frizz, who was no more interested in ranks than the others, "but yours seems pretty far down."

"You still have so many things in your career to look forward to," Fatty suggested, to put a friendlier construction on Frizz's remark.

"That's not it, boys! If you'd been paying attention better, I wouldn't have to point out that the lieutenant has one of the *lowest* ranks among the officers, whereas, among the generals, the lieutenant general has a *higher* rank than the major general."

"How is that even possible?" Mario asked in disbelief.

"The last shall be first," said Lensy. "That's a line from—" He went no further, because Micha had elbowed him again.

"I'm being promoted to sublieutenant next week, and there's going to be a crackdown here," the DPE said decisively. "If one of you finds a passport belonging to a West German citizen, it's to be turned in to me. Understood?"

"What is the name of the West German citizen?" Lensy asked. He had to know every detail.

"It goes without saying that any passport you find must be turned in to me. The lost passport in question, however, belongs to one Helene Rumpel. Boys, what is the name of the West German citizen?"

"Helene Rumpel," Mario answered. Mario had the longest hair and was therefore considered the most rebellious. Whenever Mario gave the DPE a straight answer, the patrolman could feel that he'd imposed his will at the grounds.

"Precisely. Rumpel, Helene," the DPE repeated, and the boys nodded. The DPE started to leave, but he took only three steps before something occurred to him and he came back.

"And what was that tune you were playing?" he asked ominously, groping for the Play button on the recorder; and "Moscow" started up again. Micha's heart was in his throat. The most banned of banned songs! The DPE listened for a moment and nodded connoisseurially.

"Whose recording device?" he asked. "Eh? And whose tape might this be?"

"It's actually mine," Micha said.

"Aha! I'm going to take it with me. As it happens, I like to DJ for my pals at the station." Imagining this, Micha shut his eyes in horror. He only heard the DPE calling cheerfully, as he left, "Well, boys? You'd never guess I had a hobby like that, would you?"

A week later, instead of being promoted from first sergeant to sublieutenant, the DPE was demoted to sergeant. And he began to harass Micha, constantly demanding to see his ID booklet. Every time Micha ran into him on the street, the drill was the same: "Sergeant Horkefeld, manhunt patrol, good afternoon. Identification, please."

The first few times, Micha took the words *manhunt patrol* seriously and assumed that anyone who listened to "Moscow" would sooner or later end up on the most-wanted list. Eventually he pieced together that the DPE really had played "Moscow" for his pals from the station, maybe even at the big police ball where the promotions were announced. And since "Moscow" was so fantastically illegal, there must have been a huge stink in the ballroom. Micha could picture the scene: the chief of police personally storming to the front of the ballroom to smash the loudspeakers with his truncheon, the interior minister drawing his service weapon to blast apart the tape player in the middle of the song, and the two of them then converging on the DPE to rip the brand-new sublieutenant insignia from his shoulders. Something like that, or even worse, had gone down, or so Micha was forced to conclude after observing, time and again, how hard the DPE rode him at the ID checks.

If the DPE hadn't taken the "Moscow" tape for himself,

Micha's first love letter wouldn't have fluttered onto the death strip. The matter was complicated, so it isn't easy to explain, but in the broadest sense it had to do with "Moscow." Micha wasn't even positive that the letter was actually to him, and he also wasn't positive that the letter was from the girl he'd have given his life to get a love letter from.

This girl was named Miriam, was in the parallel section of his grade, and was very obviously the school's prettiest girl. (To Micha, of course, she was the world's prettiest.) She was *the* Sonnenallee sensation. When she stepped into the street, its rhythm changed entirely. Road workers dropped their jackhammers, Western cars coming from the border checkpoint stopped to let Miriam cross in front of them, border guards whipped around their binoculars, and the laughter of West German high school classes on the observation platform died away, replaced by a reverent murmur.

Miriam was new at the school where Micha and Mario and the others went. No one had any particulars on her. To all of them, Miriam was the foreign, beautiful, enigmatic woman. Technically, Miriam was a bastard, but no one knew that, either. She was illegitimate because her father had turned too early in his car. He was driving to the registry office to meet Miriam's mother, who was eight months pregnant. The wedding was happening in Berlin, and Miriam's father didn't know his way around Berlin. He was coming from Dessau, and he took a wrong turn off the Adlergestell and drove down Baumschulenstraße, and suddenly he and his Trabi were at the Sonnenallee border crossing. He didn't realize he was at a border crossing, and so, in a rage, he got out of the car and ran around shouting, over and over, "But I need to get through!"

It often happened that cars blundered into the crossing, and they were usually sent back without ado. But Miriam's hotheaded father threw such a tantrum that the guards dealt with him more thoroughly. He was detained and interrogated for so long that he missed his appointment at the registry, and by the time he'd gotten a new appointment Miriam was born. Thus, Miriam was illegitimate.

Even before Miriam's little brother was born, she knew that her parents would get divorced. Her father wasn't right in the head—if he got locked out, he kicked open the apartment door or made a huge commotion in the street, which was unbelievably embarrassing for Miriam and her mother, on account of the neighbors. When Miriam's parents finally split up, Miriam's mother wanted to feel safe from the abusive stalking of Miriam's crazy father—and so she moved to the short end of the Sonnenallee. She assumed, correctly, that Miriam's father would be at pains to avoid the area.

Miriam's relationship with guys and men was utterly murky. Lensy said that Miriam acted like the typically deformed child of divorce—discreet, aimless, pessimistic. She was often seen climbing onto a motorbike that drove up at the very moment she stepped outside. The bike was an AWO, in other words *the* machine to have. The AWO was the only four-stroke motorcycle in the entire Eastern bloc, and it was all the more valuable for its rarity, not having been produced since the early sixties. Miriam's climbing onto an AWO made it clear to everyone at the grounds that she moved in an entirely different world. Neither Micha nor Mario or Lensy or Fatty had a motorcycle or so much as a moped; only Frizz had a bike, a folding one. And if any of them had had a moped, a motorcycle even, it would have been one of those insistently rattling two-strokes. Even a 350 Jawa, which in any case had only two cylinders, came nowhere near the deep and easy sound of the AWO. There must have been something irresistible about the AWO sound.

When Miriam heard the bike rumbling outside her building, she hurried out, greeted the driver with a quick kiss—and off she went. No one at the grounds had ever laid eyes on the AWO driver's face, because he always wore bike goggles.

"Maybe he's not her boyfriend at all," Micha said once. "Maybe he's just . . ." He couldn't think of anyone who would daily fetch the most beautiful of girls, let himself be greeted with a kiss, and not be her boyfriend.

"Maybe it's just her uncle," Mario said mockingly. Mario was smitten with Miriam himself, but unlike Micha he didn't romanticize her. "Do you want to go *out* with her, or do you want to worship her?" he asked Micha once, and Micha answered truthfully: "I guess for now I just want to worship her."

"Right, for now," Mario said. "And what comes after for now?"

"Then . . . then I want to die for her," Micha replied. It was troubling to consider how far he was from getting started with a girl if all he wanted to do was worship her and then nobly die for her.

Weeks and months went by without his ever managing to speak to Miriam, and whenever he might have had an opportunity, like when she suddenly appeared in front of him in the school-cafeteria line, he made himself scarce.

Micha did repeatedly try to extract whatever information

he could from Miriam's little brother. Everyone who was smitten with Miriam—every single boy in the upper grades—tried to pump Miriam's little brother. Miriam's little brother was only ten, but he knew exactly what his information was worth. He went so far as to accept payment for it, in the form of Matchbox cars. When someone wanted something on Miriam, the first thing her brother said was "Got a Matchy?" Word of this got around quickly, and the upperclassmen all became Matchbox experts. Their relatives in the West could only wonder why fifteen- and sixteen-year-olds wanted the Road Dragster or the Lamborghini Countach for Christmas; because Miriam's little brother wouldn't take just any car. When Lensy tried to palm off a boring frog-green Kennel Truck on him, he withheld his information. The car had to be at least a Maserati or a Monteverdi Hai, with a working suspension.

Miriam's brother was privileged in a further respect: no one dared touch him. If kids his own age were threatening to beat him up, he could count on support from the older boys, and they, too, left him alone, no matter how brazen he got. Miriam's brother was as untouchable as Miriam herself.

* * *

Micha did, once, when he was in a real predicament, try to attract Miriam's attention.

The predicament was that he'd been condemned to contribute to the political discussion. His friend Mario had artfully subtracted two letters from a hand-crafted slogan, THE PARTY IS THE WORKING CLASS'S GREATEST ASSET, that was

15

spelled out on a wall of the school lobby. Mario was snitched on; there was always a snitch who snitched on everyone. Unfortunately, Mario was on a kind of hit list. "One more thing like that, and you'll have it coming," he'd been told the previous time, when all he'd done was get caught smoking. And now he had it coming—whatever that meant. Mario wanted to go to college or at least apprentice as a car mechanic, and suddenly he was looking at a career as a concrete worker, a cutting-machine operator, or a specialist in fabrication technology. But Micha, as Mario's friend, took the fall for the missing E and T; it might have had something to do with his having just read Schiller's ode to friendship. There was also no denying that Micha wished he had a reputation for performing daring deeds. And the artful subtraction of two letters from a Red slogan was a daring deed. Alas, neither Mario nor Micha was aware that the slogan came from Lenin. The rope that was placed around a wrongdoer's neck was wound as follows: Whoever insults Lenin insults the Party. Whoever insults the Party insults the GDR. Whoever insults the GDR is opposed to peace. Whoever opposes peace must be battled—and by all appearances Micha had insulted Lenin. He was consequently sentenced by his principal, who had the punishing name Erdmute Löffeling, to prepare a *contribution to the discussion.*

Contributions to the discussion were a genuine punishment, although in fact they were a genuine honor. No one wanted to contribute to the discussion. Everyone talked their way out of it. You had to sound like you really wanted to, but, sadly, sadly, owing to unfavorable circumstances, you couldn't. "I get shy in front of a big audience." "There are absolutely people better than me." "I can't think of anything worthy enough to talk about." "I'm not a good speaker." "My mother is sick and I don't have time to prepare." "I had the honor last year." "I'm definitely losing my voice." But Micha, of course, couldn't talk his way out. Having sinned, he needed to display remorse. His contribution to the discussion was to be titled "What Quotations from the Classical Authors of Marxism-Leninism Have to Say to Us Today." Miriam still hadn't had anything to do with Micha. He was afraid that in Miriam's mind he would be "the guy who gave the Red speech" if the first impression she had of him was a speech like that. Micha needed to get to Miriam beforehand and give her the right context for him. This was his predicament.

He had two weeks, and in these two weeks there was also a school disco dance. The dance was held in the first weeks of the school year, before anyone had earned bad enough grades that they couldn't relax. Even then, the mood never got off the ground, because the dance ended at nine and only in the last half hour were the auditorium lights turned down, as in a disco. Nevertheless, the school dance seemed to Micha his one good opportunity to give Miriam a context for him.

The school dance turned out to be the worst of opportunities. All the older boys showed up, all with the same intention. The person who didn't come was Miriam. Only after boredom had reduced Micha, Mario, Frizz, Lensy, and Fatty to peeling the labels off their cola bottles did Miriam arrive. She sat down with her girlfriend, and the two of them began to chatter as if they hadn't seen each other in ten years. Miriam's friend was known behind her back as Shrapnel, because some wise guy had once said that her face must have been blasted by shrapnel. Micha knew there was no chance of enlisting

someone to approach the two girls with him and do the dancing with Shrapnel. Not even Mario was up for that; long before Miriam arrived and sat down by Shrapnel, he'd said to
Micha, "I know I owe you, but don't even think of me getting
danced on by *her*."

Micha had no choice but to man up and take care of business on his own. During a break between songs, he left his chair
and made his way across the endless expanse of the disco. As
the next song began, he asked Miriam, "Wanna dance?" He
was making an extreme effort to appear casual. But now a terrible fear shot through him, and he realized that he couldn't
have humiliated himself more wretchedly—the song starting
up was the vilest sort of Eastern bloc song. Shittiest, shittiest-
ever Czech accent. The dance floor emptied instantly. Miriam
and Shrapnel paused in their chatter, sized him up with veiled
sidelong glances, and erupted in snorts of laughter. The entire
school witnessed his disgrace. Micha stood his ground, but
Miriam and Shrapnel went back to their chattering as if he
didn't exist. There was nothing to be done but go back across
the dance floor, under the staring eyes of the entire school.
Frizz said, "That is one brave man." With this, he said what
everyone was thinking. Micha was the first person who'd ever
dared ask Miriam to dance.

After that, Micha just sat in his chair, dazed, until suddenly something was happening—an agitation spreading
through the room. Mario nudged Micha to rouse him from
his lethargy. Lensy took off his glasses and polished them,
nervously, while Fatty's jaw dropped. "But that's not possible." Miriam was dancing, and it wasn't with Shrapnel. She
was dancing with someone male. No one knew this Someone.

He'd simply walked in, with a couple of friends, and asked Miriam to dance. His friends asked other girls, the better ones, to dance. As chance would have it, they got a slow song. A *long* slow song. Quite simply *the* long slow song. A person lucky enough to dance to this song will never forget it; will henceforth divide humanity into those who've had the experience and those who haven't. The ones who've had it are the blessed, the illuminated, while the ones who haven't are sorry creatures, wronged by destiny, cheated out of a cosmic experience.

Miriam not only danced with the stranger, she started smooching with him, intensely. Micha saw it, the clique saw it, everyone saw it. Until, all of a sudden, the lights went up and there, in the auditorium, stood Erdmute Löffeling. The smoocher was wearing a T-shirt from John F. Kennedy High School: Miriam had been smooching with a West Berliner. Erdmute Löffeling threw a towering fit. The West Berliner was kicked out on the spot, Miriam was condemned to make a contribution to the discussion, and Micha became the man of the hour.

The ensuing days brought an outbreak of feverish activity among the guys in ninth and tenth grade, all with a single aim: everyone wanted to be condemned to contribute to the discussion. The effort, to be sure, was doomed from the start; two scapegoats was the limit. There were always a few career teenagers from the Free German Youth district management at the meetings, and they would have concluded that the whole school was a disaster if all anyone talked about at the FGY meetings were transgressions and *I-vow-to-improve*. Nevertheless, in the days that followed, there was a steady stream of occurrences for which, under ordinary circumstances, each student would have been condemned to contribute to the discussion. When Frizz, in physics class, was asked for the three rules of conduct in the event of an atom-bomb detonation, he answered, "First: Watch, because you're never going to see a thing like that again. Second: Drop to the ground and crawl to the nearest graveyard. But—third—do it slowly, so as not to create a panic." He was given an F, but he wasn't sentenced to contribute to the discussion. During the hand-grenade long-throw in gym class, Mario's throw landed only four meters away from him. This was intended as a pacifist statement, but Mario had to do fifteen push-ups, ten of them clapping, to build up his endurance. He wasn't sentenced to a contribution, either. Fatty let himself get caught messing with the flagpole. Taking down flags bordered on terrorism, but Fatty was merely sentenced to carry the big flag, the so-called "banner," on October 7, which turned into a real punishment, because it was pouring rain on October 7. Everyone else only showed up long enough to be counted and then slipped away, but Fatty couldn't just disappear with the banner. And the banner, heavy in any case, became even heavier in the rain. So heavy that it refused to flutter and had to be held at a lower angle, which made leverage ratios a problem for the banner-bearer. It was a real feat of strength for Fatty to hold the soaking-wet banner high enough for its emblem be seen.

So Micha remained the only person condemned to contribute to the discussion. Aside from Miriam, of course.

Their encounter took place in the dark, behind the stage in the auditorium. As usual, Miriam was late; the meeting had been going on for quite a while. The snitch was presenting an endlessly long accounting report, abounding with percentages. The numbers were more or less clearly higher than a hundred; some of the figures were also slightly below one hundred percent. There was nothing the snitch couldn't report as a percentage: grades in Russian class; early commitments for three or ten or twenty-five years of military service; anti-imperialist solidarity donations; membership in the Free German Youth, the German-Soviet Friendship Society, the German Gymnastics and Sports Association, and the Military Sports Association; class trips; subbotniks; the Masters of Tomorrow competition; library-usage rates . . . As the snitch proceeded to elucidate the school-recess milk supply in percentages (seventeen point four percent of ninth-grade students drink whole milk with two point eight percent fat, which represented an increase of two point two percent . . .), the first students were falling asleep. The only person who wasn't put to sleep by the report was Micha—but he was waiting backstage.

Then Miriam arrived, giggling and not wearing her FGY blouse, and whispered, "Oh man am I late, I'm so late. Is this even the right place?" Micha felt so overwhelmed, he wanted to say she made every place the right place, but all he could manage in his excitement was a breathless "Yeah, right place." It was dark and tight. He'd never been this close to her. Miriam looked at Micha for a moment, turned her back to him, and pulled off her T-shirt. She had nothing on underneath it. "No peeking," she whispered with a giggle, and Micha was so spellbound he forgot to breathe. Miriam took her FGY blouse from a bag and slipped into it. Before she'd finished buttoning it, she turned back to Micha. He was still paralyzed.

"So," whispered Miriam, "you put your foot in it, too?"

"What?" Micha said, not following.

"You must have gotten in trouble for something."

"Oh right, yes, of course!" Micha said, no longer whispering but speaking so loudly that he could have been heard in the auditorium if anyone had pricked up their ears a little. "I attacked Lenin, also the working class and the Party. You can imagine how that went over."

The harder Micha tried to explain the context to Miriam, the duller her reaction seemed to get. "They made an incredible fuss, they practically put me—"

"People in the West have a whole different way of kissing," Miriam interrupted, a romantic timbre in her voice, and Micha gulped and fell silent. "I really wish I could show somebody," she whispered, with a giggle. Then she stopped giggling—as if she'd had an idea. Micha had a feeling *which* idea. It was so cramped backstage, he couldn't retreat a single step. He saw her full lips gleaming moistly in the darkness. As she slowly came closer, he sensed two excitingly full breasts rising and falling in her FGY blouse, and he smelled her soft floral scent. He closed his eyes and thought *No one is going to believe this*.

At that very moment, the snitch finished her report, and Miriam was announced at the lectern. It was dark backstage but not so dark that Miriam couldn't see Micha's stricken look. "I'll show you someday!" she said with one last giggle. She stepped out onto the stage and gave a speech in which she confessed to finding guys who enlisted for three years in the army especially manly. She said she would unquestionably stay faithful to a man like that, even for three years. Erdmute Löffeling nodded approvingly. Only Micha could see that Miriam, behind her back, had crossed her fingers.

Intoxicated by Miriam's almost-kiss, Micha departed from his prepared remarks after only a few sentences. "Dear FGYers, I wish to speak to you today about the importance of being familiar with the writings of the theoreticians of the scientific worldview. Their thinking was infused with a great, undying love"—and the instant Micha spoke this word, his eyes began to shine and he was gripped by a euphoria in which he lost all control. "A love that made them strong and invincible, a love that released them, like butterflies, from the cocoon into which they'd been spun, so they could flutter free and happy through this wonderful world, through magnificent meadows full of fragrant flowers blooming in the most gorgeous colors . . ." Fatty frowned and said, in a low voice, "Did somebody put something in his food?" Mario whispered back, "If they did, I want some of it."

Micha's elation led Erdmute Löffeling to wonder aloud, in her brief welcoming address, "Is a revolutionary permitted to be passionate?" to which she immediately answered, "Yes, indeed, a revolutionary is permitted to be passionate."

Mario had to hold Micha down, because otherwise he would have jumped to his feet and shouted, eyes shining, across the auditorium, "Yes! Yes! Let's all be a little more passionate!"

After the assembly, Micha went up to Miriam and said, so that only she could hear him, "I saw you crossing your fingers during your speech."

"Oh yeah?" Miriam said. "Then I guess you and I have a secret." She left Micha standing and ran quickly for the exit.

Micha thought he heard the AWO rumbling. He hurried after Miriam, but all he got was a glimpse of her riding away on the back of the bike. Nothing could dampen his good mood, not even the DPE demanding to see his identification.

She promised me a kiss, she promised me a kiss, he rejoiced the whole way home. Aware, however, that his mother could see him from the kitchen window, he tried not to let anything show.

Inwhicheveryonetalksatonce

Micha's mother was named Doris, and she was fond of saying, "I'm the one who keeps this joint running!" Indeed she was. The "joint" also included Micha's siblings, Bernd and Sabine, both of whom were older than Micha.

Bernd was in the army, though he'd come within an inch of avoiding it. He had a very strange birthday, February 29. Probably, in the army's view, to judge from the fact that Bernd wasn't called up, every February consisted of twenty-eight days. When it was announced in the newspaper that everyone born on such-and-such dates had to report for duty, Bernd thought he could just ignore it: "I can't be expected to read the paper every day! If they're not aware of me, maybe they'll just forget me. There's no way it's ever coming out." Mrs. Kuppisch, who even back then was anxious, said, "A thing like that always comes out!"

So in spite of himself Bernd went to the army district command. He spread out his newspaper for the review committee and said, "Hello, I'm here in response to your ad." The review-committee officers didn't find this funny in the least. "No joking!" they commanded, and then snarled at him, "Other standards apply here! Not only in every regard but in more than every regard!" They threatened Bernd with *prull-tariat dictatorship* and declared that he'd already pushed the limits "not only beyond the allowable but the most allowable."

When Bernd returned from the review, all he had to say was "Those people have a really weird way of talking." But as soon as he was in the army, he picked up his own weird way of expressing himself. When he came home on leave, the Kuppisches got to know an entirely new side of him. Instead of asking, "When's dinner?" he said, "Can we get some chow on the table?" And when he was asked how the theater had been, his reply sounded something like: "After reporting for duty in the auditorium, I took up my position in row 8. No incidents of note." His family was worried, of course, but was careful not to show it. This will pass, they thought, it's just a phase.

Even with Bernd away in the army, the cramped apartment was no less cramped than ever. It was an exhausting home, Micha felt. Mr. Kuppisch was a streetcar driver and often had to rise at very early hours. Through the thin walls, Micha could hear the many sounds a man begins his day with. Because Mr. Kuppisch worked irregular shifts as a streetcar driver, Micha could also never be sure what time his father was coming home. Lensy's father, by contrast, was an engineer and returned every day at exactly five minutes to five. A paradisal situation, in Micha's view. Lensy also had no siblings, whereas Micha, besides his brother, Bernd, had a sister named Sabine, likewise older than he. She'd reached the age of having a steady boyfriend, whom she kept with her at all times. But she didn't seem to quite grasp the concept of a steady boyfriend—she always had *another* steady boy-friend. Micha didn't even bother learning the names; he just said "Sabine's latest." Whoever her latest might be, Sabine loved him so deeply and sincerely that she was forever trying to emulate him. Mr. Kuppisch once caught her filling out an application to join the Party. He hit the roof (which didn't mean much in that tiny apartment), and Sabine, by way of excuse, gestured at her latest and said, "But he's in the Party, too."

"And I'm sponsoring her application," her latest averred. "Right? I'm going to be your sponsor!"

Sabine nodded in happy anticipation, but Mr. Kuppisch put a simple end to it by taking the Party application away from Sabine, folding it a few times, and wedging it under the wobbly table.

Cramped though the apartment was, room was made for a big armchair. It was a massive, throne-like wing chair with bulging armrests and a deep, welcoming cushion. This arm-chair was customarily occupied by Uncle Heinz, their West-ern relative. Heinz must have felt good in the chair, because he often came to visit. This was the whole point of the chair.

Mr. Kuppisch read the *Berliner Zeitung*, not the *Neues Deutschland*. The former was a small paper with an advertis-ing section and lots of local news, the latter the Party's *central organ*. Mrs. Kuppisch had ascertained that the newspapers all basically ran the same things the *ND* had run the day before, and she kept trying to convince her husband to switch to the *ND*. But Mr. Kuppisch didn't want to: "I'm a long way from making myself read that crap."

"But our neighbor reads the *ND*," said Mrs. Kuppisch. "It can't be so bad."

"Yeah, and he's with the Stasi," said Mr. Kuppisch.

"What makes you think that?"

"He reads the *ND!*" Mr. Kuppisch was never at a loss for evidence that his neighbor was with the Stasi. Mrs. Kuppisch wasn't so sure about it. This led to endless arguing.

He: "Plus, he's got a telephone."

She: "But that doesn't prove anything at all!"

He: "Oh yeah? Are *we* with the Stasi?"

She: "No, obviously."

He: "And do *we* have a telephone? Eh?"

She: "No, but . . ."

Here Mrs. Kuppisch was stumped. The Kuppisches did not, in fact, have a telephone.

"All right," Mr. Kuppisch grumbled. "I'll file a petition."

"Careful, though, Horst, be careful," said Mrs. Kuppisch.

Uncle Heinz, the Western relative, had never heard of petitions. "Petition—what's that?"

"It's the only thing the leadership is still scared of," Mr. Kuppisch said emphatically, eyes blazing, as if his petitions could make the mighty tremble in their palaces. "If I go to the bathroom in the morning, and the water's off because they were fiddling with the pipes again, well, then I—"

"Yeah, a petition is really just a complaint," Micha said, to lower the temperature, and Mrs. Kuppisch lowered it further. "Complaint, complaint, what a word! As if we complain."

"Damn right we complain!" Mr. Kuppisch said stubbornly.

"No!" said Mrs. Kuppisch. "We suggest . . . or we point out . . . or we inquire . . . or we request . . . But *complain*? Us? Never!"

Uncle Heinz was Mrs. Kuppisch's brother. He, too, lived on the Sonnenallee, albeit on the long end. He was mindful of what he owed the family as their Western relative. "Look what I've smuggled in again," he always said by way of greeting, his voice hushed, his expression conspiratorial. Everything Heinz brought them was thoroughly smuggled. He put chocolate bars in his socks, he stuffed a package of gummy bears in his underpants. He never got caught. But every time he crossed the border he sweated terribly. "Heinz, it's all legal," Micha had explained to him a hundred times. "Gummy bears are okay."

Micha wished Heinz would bring him a record. Not necessarily "Moscow," but maybe the Doors. Such a step was too risky for Heinz. He knew the punishment for smuggling: "Twenty-five years in Siberia! Twenty-five years in Siberia for half a pound of coffee!"

Micha shook his head. "I've heard that story, too, but it was half a year in Siberia for twenty-five pounds of coffee."

Even Matchbox cars were too hot for Heinz. "I'd be setting myself up for, oh, what do they call it—glorifying the class enemy—if I let you see the kind of cars we have. Or say I bring you a cute little police car—that would be trivializing the enemy, and I don't feel like cutting down trees in Siberia for that! But why do you still want Matchbox cars?" Yes, why did Micha still want Matchbox cars.

Whenever Heinz visited, Mr. Kuppisch would wrestle

with the extendable table. He could never make it work. And yet he never tired of extolling the practicality of such a table. Even the crank that controlled the table's height seemed practical to him. He maintained that folding bikes and collapsible toothbrushes were practical as well. Any bad design that promised to save space and was ugly was certified as "practical" by Mr. Kuppisch. There was something fanatical about the optimism with which he grappled with his practical objects. "Just a second, oh, I've almost got it," he always said. But it was never just a second.

Every time Heinz assumed his place in the tiny living room's huge armchair and let his gaze wander the room, he would sigh and say, "This is an absolute death chamber!" Years ago, after discovering asbestos behind the radiator, he'd raised the alarm: "Asbestos, you've got asbestos! It causes lung cancer!"

Mr. Kuppisch, who'd never heard the word *asbestos*, cried: "I'll file a petition!"

Mrs. Kuppisch cried: "Careful, though, Horst, be careful!"

As always, Mr. Kuppisch didn't file a petition, and little by little the asbestos was forgotten, even though Heinz reminded them, with a sigh, every time he came to visit: "An absolute death chamber!" Micha couldn't help comparing his parents with the Rosenbergs in Sing Sing, and sometimes he tried to imagine what his parents would look like in the death chamber. (His father would probably still be shouting from the electric chair, "I'll file a petition! Don't you see? I'm innocent!")

One day, when his brother-in-law had smuggled in a pair of ladies' shoes stuffed with newsprint, and Mr. Kuppisch had smoothed out the crumpled *Bild-Zeitung*, his face went pale. "Here," he said, pointing to a fat headline:

DEAD 15 YEARS LATER
KILLER ASBESTOS CAUSES CANCER!

"Death chambers!" Uncle Heinz shouted. "That's what I've been telling you!"

Mrs. Kuppisch began to calculate.

Mr. Kuppisch, Micha, and Sabine were calculating, too. "We moved in here . . ."

"Wait a second . . ."

"Let's see . . . fifteen years ago . . ."

"No, it's more than that . . ."

"No way. Not if we count vacations . . ."

". . . and all the times we're out of the house—Micha, Sabine, you're in school six hours a day, right?"

"It doesn't quite add up to . . . fifteen years."

Fifteen years. There it stood in fat letters, in the wrinkled *Bild* on the table: After fifteen years, killer asbestos causes deadly lung cancer.

"I'm filing a petition," Mr. Kuppisch said in a shaky voice.

"Careful, though, Horst, be careful! Don't tell them where you heard it. Do you think they'll let Misha study in Moscow if we're constantly complaining?"

"He wants to study in Moscow?" Heinz asked angrily. "He ought to be at Harvard, at the Oxford Sorbonne! You only go to Russia with a machine gun on your arm or a ball on your ankle."

"Heinz, not in front of the boy," Mrs. Kuppisch hissed.

Micha wasn't at all sure he wanted to study in Moscow; his mother had decided for him. She was the one responsible for such decisions. To study in Moscow, Micha would have to take prep classes at a special school called the Red Monastery. And to get into the Red Monastery he had to be outstanding in every respect. He had to have outstanding grades, outstanding career goals, an outstanding political attitude, and outstanding behavior, and he had to demonstrate outstanding commitment, surround himself with outstanding friends, and come from a no less outstanding family.

"We need to maintain an ex*empl*ary reputation," said Mrs. Kuppisch, who knew how things were done. "Horst! From now on, you're reading the *ND*, not the *Berliner*."

"What? The *ND*? It's so big!"

"Exactly. Everyone can *see* you reading it."

"But it's so cramped in here—how am I even supposed to open the *ND*?"

"Sit by the window, where everyone can see you. That way, when the Stasi come to the neighbors and ask about us, they'll say we're a home where the *ND* is read. Everything will be in order, and Misha can go to the Red Monastery and study in Moscow."

"The Stasi won't *come* to the neighbors, because the neighbors *are* the Stasi," said Mr. Kuppisch.

"Yeah, yeah, you think you're so sure," said Mrs. Kuppisch.

"Of course I'm sure! I saw with my own eyes how they got their Wartburg's brakes fixed in less than a week. Didn't I? Can you explain that to me?"

Micha had once gone so far as to ask his neighbor, point-blank, where he worked. The look he received from the neighbor made him feel he'd asked an indecent question. Playing innocent, he explained: "I'm only asking on account of my career choice. When a person doesn't have to leave the house until eight thirty, and his wife doesn't have to work . . . I mean: sleeping late and still earning enough for two people—I'm interested in that." Needless to say, he didn't get an answer.

Micha in fact had no idea what he wanted to be. Hanging out at the grounds, he heard Lensy and Mario discussing their new favorite topic. It had dawned on Lensy that there was no such thing as an unpolitical college major—and why bother with a high school diploma if there weren't any unpolitical college majors?

Mario: "What about architecture?"

Lensy: "So you can build houses the way the Party wants them to look?"

According to Lensy, not even ancient and early European history were unpolitical: all you learned about there was how people in the past had already been yearning for the Party.

But these discussions usually ended when a tourist bus came rolling across the border and into the East. Mario and Micha would run up to the bus, stretch out their hands like beggars, widen their eyes, and cry out: "Hungry! Hungry!"

The tourists, appalled by conditions behind the Iron Curtain, took pictures, and after the bus was gone Mario and Micha would laugh themselves half dead, imagining how their pictures would be shared around in Pittsburgh, Osaka, or Barcelona. No one else at the grounds felt like joining in. Mario and Micha, meanwhile, gave ever more exaggerated and theatrical performances—they doubled over, rooted desperately in trash cans, pretended to collapse, or scuffled over a scrap of lettuce outside the vegetable store. Their hope, of course, was to be seen doing their *Hungry! Hungry!* show by Miriam and make her laugh, maybe even inspire some admiration in her. But Miriam was never around when a tourist bus came rolling across the border.

Dance hall days

Since Miriam's promise of a kiss, Micha had run into her only once. They walked for a while down the street, and Micha was at a total loss for what to talk about. Recalling the asbestos, he finally said, "I don't have much longer to live." When they went their separate ways, all he said was "Bye."

In return for an orange Monteverdi Hai, Micha had obtained from Miriam's little brother the information that Miriam had signed up for dance school. He was careless enough to report this at the grounds—whereupon Mario, Lensy, and Fatty signed up for dance school. Micha himself was disinclined, because he didn't know how to dance. Mario told him, "That's the whole point! Nobody at dance school knows how to dance." Obviously, Micha didn't want to be hanging out at the grounds while the others went to dance class with Miriam. But he couldn't bring himself to sign up. He did go to the dance school and see, on the studio blackboard, that the teacher's name was Mrs. Schlooth—but he didn't sign up. Instead, realizing that he could see into the school through the windows of a stairwell that faced it, he hid there and covertly observed the goings-on in the studio.

He saw two opposing rows of chairs in which twenty or so neatly combed gentlemen sat across from an equal number of smartly dressed ladies. In between them, on the dance floor, the dance teacher was illustratively holding up a knife and a fork. Apparently the dance school didn't teach just dancing but manners in general. Micha didn't think his own manners were the worst, since he always washed his hands before eating and didn't wipe his nose on his sleeve.

Mrs. Schlooth, the dance teacher, was a peroxided, significantly overweight lady in stiletto heels who was assisted by two young male ballroom dancers in tight feminine pantsuits. Until this moment, Micha had never actually seen a gay man; in the past, it had always been someone saying that so-and-so was gay. Now, seeing the two ballroom dancers, he so fully grasped the concept of gayness, he christened them the Ballroom Dancing Pansies.

Mrs. Schlooth, demonstrating a new dance, was doing a few steps with one of the Dancing Pansies and then a few steps with the other. It was obvious that, even in spike heels, Mrs. Schlooth knew how to manage the momentum of her not inconsiderable mass. As she exhaustively explained the dance, still embraced by one of the Dancing Pansies, Micha could see the other Dancing Pansy watching them like someone practicing a jealous glare.

When the demonstration was over, one of the Dancing Pansies went over to a console where a stack of records had been readied and put one on the turntable. Then places were taken. The gentlemen had to get up and ask the ladies to dance. This was the moment when Micha understood that going to dance school would also mean being very, very close to Miriam, and that if his fingers were cold, his hands clammy, his breath bad, or his armpits sweaty, there would be no hiding it.

While the students practiced the new dance, which looked every bit as ridiculous as Micha had imagined, Mrs. Schlooth corrected the couples individually. The Dancing Pansies kept cutting in and separating couples, each of them dancing with one of the partners, by way of hands-on instruction. As a result, one of the twenty gentlemen was always dancing with one of the Dancing Pansies. This was a bit much, Micha felt. And when the couples were reunited they didn't dance the slightest bit better. No surprise there: if Micha had had to dance with a man, he would have been too tense to learn a thing.

Mrs. Schlooth made everyone change partners after every song, the gentlemen moving from one lady to the next. This meant that each student, in the course of an hour, had approximately twelve different dance partners, including the Dancing Pansies. When the class was over and Micha saw the students on the street, saying their goodbyes and dispersing, he thought maybe dance classes weren't so bad after all—and signed up.

For a while, it was even worse than he'd thought. At Mrs. Kuppisch's behest, he dressed up for dance school. The only dressy thing he had was his suit from his coming-of-age ceremony. In the year since then, he'd grown nearly five inches, and his much too small suit never failed to elicit special jeering from the observation platform across the border. The DPE, who'd been riding Micha since "Moscow" had gotten him demoted, went out of his way to check Micha's ID in the vicinity of the observation platform, which made things even worse; the ID check was accompanied by applause and shouts of "That's right, Officer, don't let him get away with it!" and "Arrest him! Arrest him! Looks totally criminal!" and "Book him! Question him! Torture him!" This happened before *every* dance class. It was a difficult time for Micha.

At the first session of dance school, the gentlemen sat down across from the ladies, and Miriam, of course, was hungrily eyed by all the gentlemen. Everything was more or less as Micha had expected. As Mrs. Schlooth demonstrated the first steps, he was again impressed by her elegance—a fat lady floating around with such seeming ease, she might have weighed nothing at all.

Then came the crucial moment. Mrs. Schlooth announced: "The gentlemen will now rise, approach a lady at an unhurried pace, and ask for a dance with a simple nod." The moment was an eye-opener for Mrs. Schlooth. When Micha had signed up for dance school, she'd still been marveling that, as she put it, "We don't have a 'couples problem' this time." Usually, more ladies than gentlemen were willing to take dance lessons. Sometimes the imbalance was so extreme that a lady was admitted only if she brought along a gentleman; there might even be a fee reduction for gentlemen, at least for the ones who'd already taken the class and wanted to repeat. Micha's class, however, didn't have a "couples problem," not in the usual sense. The reason became evident to Mrs. Schlooth the instant she prompted the gentlemen to ask the ladies for their first dance. It was as if she'd commanded a full-scale assault on Miriam. The entire line of gentlemen converged on a single point. There was pushing and shoving, people falling. Micha was the first to get to Miriam. He was the first to put his arm around her waist, take her by the hand, and succeed in looking into her eyes. He hadn't imagined how happy it would make him just to hold her. He registered the softness of her body, the evenness of her breathing, the scent of her hair. But then the dancing started, and the romance was over. Micha had no idea how to dance. He kept stepping on Miriam's feet, and after two minutes she couldn't wait to get away from him. Her wish was granted: according to procedure, Micha had to relinquish her at the end of the dance. Miriam's next partner was Mario. He was no better. And so it went—everyone wanted to dance with Miriam, everyone stomped on her feet.

Week after week, the dance lesson played out the same way: first a mob scene, centered on Miriam, and then, after each dance, the next partner stepped up according to his place in the row. Before the class even started, there was scuffling for the seat directly across from Miriam, because it afforded the shortest path to her—until Micha revolutionized the process and secured the hour's *last* dance with Miriam. He was smart enough to keep his new tactic to himself, particularly his way of ensuring that he always got the very last dance.

He remembered observing, while spying from the stairwell outside, that a stack of records was prepared for every dance lesson. To find out how many songs would be played, all he had to do before the lesson was count the records—and then, starting with Miriam, count back along the ladies' row to calculate which one he needed to start with to get the last dance with Miriam. While twenty gentlemen fought over Miriam, Micha walked at an unhurried pace to the lady he'd counted back to. If there were nine songs for practicing the foxtrot, Micha would go all out with eight of them—he didn't care if he mishandled his partners, stepped on them, even dropped them. Whenever there was a crash or a thud in the middle of a dance, everyone knew that Micha's partner was on the floor again. Only judo class was worse. Micha developed a terrible reputation; it was whispered that he "abused girls." His dance partners would show one another the bruises he'd given them. Micha considered them his practice material. "Anyone who goes to dance school has to know what they're getting into," he said. Not until the last dance of each lesson, with Miriam, did he try to be good. And he actually succeeded. One reason might have been that he was the only gentleman able to overcome his horror of the Dancing Pansies and get something useful from dancing with them.

In the end, Miriam elected Micha as the best of the male dancers. After the final class, the tango class, she asked him if he'd like to be her date at the graduation ball. Which was exactly as Micha had envisioned it.

While rejoicing in the success of his calculations, however, he'd overlooked the fact that in the foregoing weeks he'd begun the hour with Shrapnel four times, doing the waltz, the boogie-woogie, the Charleston, and the rumba. Shrapnel now believed that *she* was Micha's object of desire and he just hadn't worked up the courage to show it.

Fifty Western short

Frizz didn't go to dance school. Things like that didn't interest him. Nothing else interested him, either, except music. And music itself only interested him if it was by the Rolling Stones. While his friends from the grounds were at dance school, he endeavored to get his hands on *Exile on Main Street*, the '72 Stones double album. Frizz only wanted it for taping, but the quality had to be flawless, from an English pressing, no Yugo shit, still less an Indian pressing. And he'd heard of a guy, Frankie, who had every Stones album. By all accounts, if Frankie wasn't doing time for assault again, he was sitting at home and listening to the Stones at full blast. Frizz went to Frankie's, and, sure enough, heard "Paint It Black" from the courtyard. It wasn't from *Exile*, but almost. Frizz climbed the stairs and stopped outside a door with the Stones playing behind it. He rang the bell and knocked, but "Brown Sugar" was blasting, then "Gimme Shelter," "Have You Seen Your Mother, Baby," and "Honky Tonk Women," and Frankie didn't open the door. Trying not to think about

Frankie's criminal profile, Frizz pounded on the door as hard as he could, first with his fists and then resorting to kicking it. At some point, the door was opened. Or rather, ripped open. A huge brute with tattoos and a long criminal record was standing in the doorway, staring at him. Frizz bravely inquired about *Exile*. The tattooed brute continued to stare, his lower lip drooping, and Frizz batted his eyelashes winningly. He thereby obtained the address of a hippie who lived in Strausberg and was now evidently the possessor of *Exile*. "Lost it gambling drunk," Frankie croaked, while Frizz judiciously retreated.

Frizz rode his folding bike to Strausberg to look for the Strausberg hippie. He lived in a construction trailer. The trailer was parked between a pair of trees with a hammock strung between them, and lying in the hammock was the Strausberg hippie. He was listening to music and reading a book with the title *The Fan Man*. Frizz wouldn't venture into the construction trailer, because the entire trailer floor was awash in album covers. To move around in the trailer would be to wade in records—and this was sacrilege to Frizz.

"Hey man, who are you?" said the Strausberg hippie.

"Got your address from Frankie—guy with the tattoos," Frizz said.

"Yeah, man, know him, man, lives in Berlin, man, crazy city, man, got a TV tower in the middle of it. So, man, what brings you to me?"

"Well, you've got *Exile on Main Street*."

"No, man, wrong way of looking at it, I mean, yeah, I got it from Frankie, but man, you know, I traded it for Zappa and Zeppelin. Not saying it sucks, *Exile*, but things gotta keep moving, gotta circulate, like this wonderful book here, I took it from hallowed hands, man, hallowed hands. So, yeah, man, I got a shitload of records, but you're not gonna find *Exile* here."

Frizz was at least able to learn whom the hippie had traded records with. "It was Bergmann, man, know what I'm saying?" Since Bergmann lived in Berlin, Frizz got on his folding bike again and pedaled back to Berlin.

When the school's gym teacher learned how effortlessly Frizz could bike long distances, he showed up at Frizz's door with a junior coach. It was a comical situation: two men in tracksuits trying to recruit Frizz for Olympic training. Frizz talked his way out of it. "I have absolutely no Olympic ambitions. Honestly, training's not my thing. Pole-vaulting's as far as I'll go."

"Why pole-vaulting?" the sports-club coach asked, surprised.

"Because it means practicing clearing three meters forty-five," Frizz said. Neither of the men understood what he was suggesting. The Wall was three meters and forty-five centimeters high, and according to Lensy the GDR prohibited any sport that could be used to flee the country. Thus, no one was permitted to sail or to surf on the Baltic. Kites and paragliding were likewise forbidden, lest anyone have ideas of flying to the West from a high-rise near the border. Lensy knew this for a fact. He was well informed about things that nobody else was even aware of, despite how pertinent they were to everyone.

Needless to say, Frizz didn't become a pole-vaulter—he figured it was only a matter of time before pole-vaulting was banned anyway. Frizz was on the trail of *Exile on Main Street*—which, if the Strausberg hippie was to be believed, was in the possession of someone named Bergmann.

Bergmann was an anxious sort. Among other things, he lived in fear of house searches, and so he kept his records, which he considered daaaangerous, in unsuspicious sleeves. An Eric Burdon LP resided in the sleeve of Bach's *The Well-Tempered Clavier*. Bachman-Turner Overdrive was camouflaged by the record jacket of a brass band. To conceal *Exile*, he'd gone so far as to purchase two recordings of the Alexandrov Ensemble, because *Exile* was a double album and required two sleeves. His girlfriend was surprised to see a Soviet army choir among the new additions to his record collection.

And then Bergmann went into the army, where he fell victim to one misfortune after another. First, a smoke grenade exploded on him in the latrine. He lost his leave privileges for that. Then he gave the wrong directions to a tank, causing it to back over a bust of Gagarin and demolish it. He lost his privileges for that as well. Finally, Bergmann managed to forget his bazooka in a pub, leaving it standing there like an umbrella. For this, he not only lost his leave privileges but spent ten days in the brig. His girlfriend at home had already uncorked the wine and was waiting for him, wearing nothing but her slip, she was so sex-starved. But once again, instead of Bergmann, a telegram carrier came to the door. Bergmann's girlfriend worked herself into such a rage that she finished off the wine and, cursing the army, still wearing her slip, smashed Bergmann's two army recordings to smithereens. Blinded by tears of fury, she couldn't see what she was actually smashing.

Frizz wept, too, when he learned the fate of the only copy of *Exile on Main Street* to be found far and wide.

His tears didn't dry until he heard about Edge, a rake-thin record dealer who supposedly hung out under an S-Bahn trestle, like a ghost, and sold records that he'd obtained through one sinister channel or another. Some people said he was with the Stasi, others that he spied for three different agencies all at once; there were also those who said he procured women willing to go topless at diplomatic parties. Still others maintained that he merely chauffeured low-level embassy staff to the Baltic and received Western goods in return. This was quite possible, since he was only under the trestle between six and seven on Tuesday evenings, and who gets driven to the Baltic then?

Arriving at the trestle at the specified time, Frizz did in fact see a thin dude loitering with a rectangular bag and staring into space. Although the sky was overcast, the dealer wore sunglasses. This made a big impression on Frizz, so he maintained a respectful distance from the action while he tried to figure out what the conventions were. First, an interested party had to place an order, to which Edge then responded with unbelievably condescending commentary. "You want *Dylan*? That is so *yesterday* over there." "Bee Gees? Quacking eunuchs, faggified disco shit." "The Stones you can forget about, now that Brian Jones is dead." Edge could afford to be arrogant because he really could get everything. When Frizz placed his order for *Exile on Main Street*, an English pressing, still in its shrink-wrap, Edge said: "Of course it'll be shrink-wrapped. You think I'm still listening to that junk?"

Three weeks later, Edge did indeed have a shrink-wrapped

Exile in his bag, but he wanted three hundred East German marks from Frizz.

"Three hundred marks?" Frizz said, aghast. "I'd have to spend four weeks of vacation working."

"I should hope so! If the Stones spent four weeks in the studio, the least you can do is spend four weeks working to pay for it."

"But I don't have three hundred marks."

"How about fifty Western marks?" Edge said.

"I don't have fifty Western, either!" Frizz said.

Edge exhaled contemptuously and let the shrink-wrapped double album vanish back inside his bag.

"Then you're fifty Western short," he said coldly.

Frizz swallowed and promised to come back when he had the dough. I believe that, even at the time, Mario predicted that Frizz would never listen to his *Exile*, because he'd never be able to bring himself to tear open the shrink-wrap. "Wanting something is much more interesting than having it," Mario said. "Women, for example." And everyone who heard him nodded and thought enviously: Man, the things he knows!

* * *

The music back then was good, much better than today. So says everyone who had a tape recorder back then. All anyone did back then was make tapes. There was only one word and the word was *tape*. Someone had the record, and then it was taped to cassette. Nowadays, the whole world uses CDs. They're better, but records have a lot more charm. When a CD skips, it sounds hectic and rights itself aggressively, whereas a record's way of jumping is rather musical and soothing, at least on a sixth or seventh hearing. Records had to be handled gently, they might get scratched, they were so sensitive. Records gave you the feeling that you were dealing with something precious. The way Frizz handled his records, his solemn way of drawing them out of their sleeves, touching them only in the center and at the edge: he even held the jackets by their edges . . . Lensy taped his own English pressings on his ZK 240 and then, because he was convinced that the needle would wear out his records, listened only to the tapes. Mario played his imports only when he was by himself, so that nobody could bump into his record player. He even walked on tiptoe, afraid that his footsteps would make the needle jump and scratch the record. And yet there were always records available for taping. People would gather and tape one or two or three LPs, sometimes more. They didn't have to know each other—it was enough that they liked the same music. They could talk or just listen to the music, and they had all the time in the world. They could feel what it was like to be a man, and the music in the background was always strong.

Clay or putty, that is the question

Despite having a Western relative, Micha didn't own a single record from the West. Records couldn't be smuggled in underpants, and Uncle Heinz wasn't the type for adventures like a false-bottomed suitcase. All a border guard had to do was leaf through his passport more thoroughly than usual, and Uncle Heinz would regret the damnably high risks he took for his poor relatives. Once, when the border guard wagged Heinz's passport at him, his heart almost stopped. "You know what I think?" the guard asked, looking at the many entry stamps. "You know what I think? A person who comes here as often as you do—you know what I think?"

Heinz's heart was in his throat, and all he could do was shake his head. He was afraid of being caught with the roll of cookies he'd taped to his calf. The guard took him into the customs hut, and Heinz thought: This is the end. Nothing but hard time from here on out. He went so far as to hold out his hands for the cuffs. Better to confess everything on the spot.

"A person who comes here as often as you do," the guard said, lowering his voice confidentially, "is undoubtedly a friend of our system!"

Heinz nodded, to be on the safe side. The guard whispered, with a meaningful look, "I'm going to show you something. But—shhh." He threw back a sheet to reveal a confiscated Japanese four-component stereo system with three-way bass-reflex boxes, a huge receiver with station presets, AFC, separate bass and treble controls, manual modulation for every channel, selector switches for mono/stereo and ferric/chromium-oxide, any number of function and band-range buttons, and no fewer than four on/off switches. The border guard struck a triumphant pose by the sound system and proudly asked, "Well?"

Heinz didn't know what to say, but no response was expected. "Look at this thing!" the guard said. "Way too complicated! And this is the sort of thing they make over there! We, on the other hand . . ."

Here the guard swept his arm toward a "Fichtelberg" radio that was leading a sad little existence among some failing potted plants. The "Fichtelberg" had four buttons, three large and one small; one dial; and one speaker.

"That's the ticket," the guard said proudly. "I'm telling you, that is something a workingman can deal with. Look here: one switch for the power *and* the volume—the most economical use of materials! And the speaker is built right in—not like that thing over there. You can't even use that thing without special speakers. Which add to the cost and take up more space!"

Heinz, who a minute earlier had imagined himself disappearing in Siberia, now sensed that there had been a misunderstanding, albeit in his favor: as a putative admirer of the GDR, he was being kept up to date on its latest achievements. He wondered if the Kuppisches could ever appreciate what it meant for him to cross the border, time after time, with the illegal gifts he'd affixed to his body with such meticulous care. Pondering their exact placement for weeks. None of the Kuppisches would ever know how it felt to be Uncle Heinz facing a border guard. Not that Heinz would have wanted to trade places with the Kuppisches and their life in the Zone, but they didn't have the faintest idea what he endured every time he crossed the border, and Heinz didn't think this was right.

The border guard had by no means finished extolling the merits of the "Fichtelberg" radio, but Heinz was in a hurry to escape the overheated hut, where a ceiling tile had burst open and asbestos was sifting down.

"You can get cancer from that," Heinz said.

This put the guard in an even better mood. "Yeah, those are the problems that people in the West have." He widely opened a mouth in which it looked as if an oral-medicine class had practiced filling cavities. "Han hou helieve it? Hesterners hink it hauses hancer." Puffing himself up, he handed Heinz his passport and clapped him on the shoulder. "But I've never had cancer. While we're advancing socialism, your people are worrying about cancer, or building radios that nobody knows how to use. Ha ha, they don't have a chance!"

Heinz nodded and considered raising his fist as a parting gesture, but he decided against it because it might be seen as a threat. He'd never understood to begin with why communists greeted each other with raised fists.

Sabine's latest, her Party sponsor, might have been able to explain it, but he was now her late latest. Sabine's latest latest was in theater, a stagehand with ambitions. He wanted to direct. Though he still had a long way to go, he was already speaking of "my actors" and how actors were mere clay in the hands of the director. Mr. Kuppisch asked, "Why clay? Why not *putty*?"

As Heinz carefully climbed the stairs, with the roll of cookies in his pants leg, he heard Sabine declaiming from *Macbeth*, "That tend on mortal thoughts, unsex me here . . ." She'd been working on this one line for twenty minutes, but because she was in the bathtub her delivery kept succumbing to contextual dissonance.

Almost invariably, when Heinz visited his sister's family, something was happening that shocked him. This time, seeing his sister was enough to take his breath away. Mrs. Kuppisch was putting herself together at the mirror, but she seemed to have aged twenty years in one leap. Mr. Kuppisch, engaged in desperate struggle with the extendable table, grimly commented: "Every other man's wife tries to make herself look younger, but apparently mine wants to look older."

When Heinz had recovered from his shock, he pointed at the killer asbestos behind the radiator and said to Mr. Kuppisch, "Be happy you get to see her like this. She's never going to live to be as old as she looks, and even if she does, you won't be alive to see it."

Mrs. Kuppisch couldn't bear this topic. "Heinz, stop it, all you do is make Misha crazy."

Micha protested. "Mom, why do you keep saying *Misha*? My name is Micha."

"I don't see the harm. Misha is Russian. Don't you want to study in the Soviet Union?"

"That's no reason to call me Misha. It's not like I call you Momushka."

"It's never a bad thing if people think we're friends of the Soviet Union," said Mrs. Kuppisch.

"Even so! Not Misha! It sounds like . . ."

"Like a mishmash," Heinz said.

Sabine interrupted her rehearsal of *Macbeth* and shouted from the bathroom, "You need to call him Miiiiisha, with Rrrrussian feelink," sounding as Russian as she could. "Like Puuushkin. Or Cheeeyekov."

"*Raz, dva, tri*—Russian we will never be!" Heinz shouted back in the direction of the bathroom.

"Heinz! Not in front of the boy!"

"Oh, why not?" Heinz said. "If Ivan's regime won't even let you have a phone, you shouldn't be sending him to Russia. How's he supposed to call you when he's in his log cabin, surrounded by wolves?"

Sabine emerged from the bathroom with her stagehand, drying her hair, and took her cue from the only word she'd caught. "We're never getting a telephone."

"My hairdresser just got a telephone because of her sugar problem," Mrs. Kuppisch said; and Heinz took it the wrong way.

"Do you need sugar?" he whispered. "I can smuggle some in."

"No, she has diabetes, she needs a phone when she gets her insulin thingy."

"I'll write a petition!" Mr. Kuppisch declared, grabbing

53

a piece of paper. He uncapped a pen—and then hesitated. "What illness do we have, though?"

Micha thought: We're all brain-damaged.

"Let's think about it," Mr. Kuppisch said, rapping on the table. "Don't we have some impressive kind of illness?"

"Lung cancer," Heinz suggested.

"No one here has lung cancer!" Mrs. Kuppisch said. "Although I do have a pollen allergy."

"That's all?" the stagehand asked.

"Yes, just a pollen allergy," said Mrs. Kuppisch.

"Won't fly," Mr. Kuppisch said sadly. "*How can it be that every one of us is healthy?*"

"It's a scandal!" Heinz said. "In the Free World, people with pollen allergies have their own hotline, and under communism people with allergies can't even get a telephone."

"What kind of hotline?" Mr. Kuppisch wanted to know.

"Well, you know, what the various pollen levels are," Heinz said. "Poplar or linden . . . It's like with honey. Over here, honey is just honey, but in the West we have wild honey, acacia honey, clover honey . . ."

"You're telling me people over there are allergic to some pollens and not others?" Mr. Kuppisch couldn't believe it. He'd never imagined that Western individualism expressed itself to such degrees of refinement.

"Exactly," Heinz said.

Mr. Kuppisch marveled, openmouthed, and looked around at everyone. "You see?"

Here the stagehand spoke up. "Brecht or Heiner Müller would approach this dialectically. If they had a pollen allergy, they'd file a petition and demand a pollen hotline—even if they didn't have a telephone."

"Yeah, so?" Mr. Kuppisch said grumpily. "What would Brecht get out of it? There'd be a hotline, but he still wouldn't have a telephone. So much for the dialectic."

"Not quite!" the stagehand exulted. "If there were a pollen line, Brecht would file another petition: *Because* there's a pollen line, now he needs to have a phone!"

"How so?"

"Well, what's the point of a hotline if people with pollen allergies don't have phones?"

What the stagehand was proposing was so compelling, no one could argue with him. Finally Mr. Kuppisch said, with an air of resignation, "It's not like anybody who isn't Stasi is getting a phone anyway."

While the Stasi neighbors were creating annoyances for Mr. Kuppisch, Mrs. Kuppisch took center stage, always in the role of the devoted mother who toed the party line. For example, she actually did subscribe to the *ND*, not to read it every morning but to let it be seen sticking out of the mailbox every morning. She put scrap paper in the mailbox to keep the *ND* from fitting all the way in. People passing the boxes couldn't help noticing that the Kuppisches were an *ND* family.

When another youth festival was approaching, Mrs. Kuppisch intercepted her Stasi neighbor in the stairwell, taking care to make the encounter seem accidental. "I'm glad I ran into you," she said. "Could you maybe loan us two air mattresses for guest quartering, now that there's another youth festival?" She stumbled a bit on the words *guest quartering* and *youth festival*; Mrs. Kuppisch had no previous history of dedication to the great common cause. The words *air mattress*, by contrast, rolled off her tongue so smoothly that an attentive listener might have gathered that she was on intimate terms with the paraphernalia of poolside fun. Mrs. Kuppisch was struck by this herself, and so she tried again. "These youth festivals are really *such* a nice thing," she called out to her neighbor, who was wordlessly digging out two air mattresses, "especially for young people! Sometimes, for their sake, you just have to squeeze together a little, even in a cramped apartment, don't you think?" Mrs. Kuppisch was thinking: How's *that* for a good socialist family? Go ahead and report it! Out loud, she said: "Our guest quartering will definitely be comfortable."

She was devising further sentences containing the words *youth festival* and *guest quartering* when Micha and Mario came up the stairs. Mrs. Kuppisch greeted her son loudly enough for the Stasi neighbor to hear: "Misha! How lovely that you're here, dinner's ready, I made solyanka—your favorite!"

Mario was all over it. "*Solyanka?*" he asked with an angry look. Micha felt exposed by his mother; he was *not* solyanka-loving Misha, especially not in front of Mario. "First the Red Monastery, and now, what, you can't get enough Russian chow? You're turning into a real Red Russian asshole!"

Mario was in an extremely irritable place. He'd had to lose his long hair. After swearing a thousand times that he would never do it, he'd done it. He hadn't even been overtly pressured. He'd cut off his long hair because, for his moped driver's exam, he'd drawn the infamous examiner whose life's work was to fail anyone, truly anyone, who had long hair. The examiner's methods weren't free of malice. Before starting a test, he would secretly disconnect the brake light, so that he could fail the long-haired examinee for not having confirmed, prior to the test, that his vehicle was in proper operating condition. Mario had already failed once; he'd been sent to the test track with his fuel tap closed, driven a few meters, and stalled in the middle of an intersection. When Mario found out that he was being retested by the same infamous examiner, he stopped in a dark hallway beforehand, put on his motorcycle helmet, and cut off all the hair that spilled out from it. He passed the exam, but hairstylewise he was now the lowest of the low, and when he encountered Mrs. Kuppisch in the stairwell, calling Misha to his solyanka, he recognized her as little as she recognized him. Mrs. Kuppisch continued to look as if she'd aged twenty years.

The next time Heinz came to visit, he, too, looked nothing like himself. In the space of five weeks, he'd starved himself down from a hundred and sixty-six pounds to a hundred and thirty. He'd eaten nothing, "less than in a Siberian gulag," as he described it, and had lifted weights every day. "I sweated more than I would breaking rocks in Siberia." Heinz was now so light that even the cushion springs sounded different when he sat down in his armchair.

"Goodness, Heinz, you scarecrow, come sit at the table," Mrs. Kuppisch said, worried. She pushed aside Mr. Kuppisch, who was trying, yet again, to make the extendable table do its thing.

"Heinz, do you have a tapeworm?" Micha asked, shocked by the sight of his uncle.

"Nope," Heinz said, and he began to undress. "I smuggled something!"

Under his suit, which hung limply on his body, he was wearing another suit, which looked as if it had been sprayed onto him. "This is for you," he said to Micha, with ceremony. "So you can dress to impress at your dance school. And now I intend to pig out like you wouldn't believe!" He gave a hearty laugh. "Try it on, I want to see if it fits," he called to Micha, his mouth full. "You can't imagine . . . the number of times I've been thinking in the last few weeks . . . I am truly going to stuff myself . . . the minute I get your suit smuggled in!"

Micha nodded. He didn't have the heart to tell Heinz that he could have brought the suit over legally. And from then on, long after Heinz had returned to a hundred and sixty-six pounds and his old suit fit him again, Micha never neglected to celebrate his Western relative for his heroic smuggling of the suit.

Micha thus not only had the best-looking partner at the dance-school graduation ball, he also had the best-looking suit. It was so sharply cut, there wasn't even any heckling from the observation platform when he set out for the ball.

Miriam wore a dark blue velvet evening dress, and Mario and Lensy and Fatty were likewise better dressed than they'd been in a long while or would soon be again. They'd even shined their shoes. Once again, eighty shiny shoes were spinning on the parquet floor, among them the shoes of Mrs. Schlooth and the two Dancing Pansies. But the It couple was Micha and Miriam. Micha was also the best dancer. He led Miriam lavishly around the parquet, and he could feel, with each dance, that she was letting him lead her more and more—because she felt safe with him. For the first time in his life, he was glimpsing what it meant to be a man, daring to be there for a woman *as a man*. Micha, whose eyes ordinarily shied from direct contact, tonight felt sucked in by Miriam's gaze. It was a revelation how much could be experienced by simply gazing.

Miriam enjoyed looking into Micha's eyes, not letting him be aware of anything but her. He didn't even hear the roar of an AWO pulling up outside the ballroom. It was during the tango, of all things—the dance that Micha was best at. Beneath the strict rhythms of the famous "La Cumparsita," the motor of an AWO idled calmly and steadily. As soon as the dance was over, Miriam excused herself from Micha. "When it can't get any nicer," she said, "it's time to stop." Everyone saw her leave him standing there, and no one would have wanted to be Micha at that moment. Until now, he'd been the prince of the evening. Regaining his senses, he ran out to the street and called after her: "When it can't get any nicer, you can also keep doing it!" But she was riding away, hugging the AWO's driver tightly, sitting sidesaddle on account of her evening dress. She was beyond hearing that Micha had called anything after her.

When Micha returned to the ballroom, a broken man, everyone stood and stared at him. A waltz was playing, and Shrapnel was already plotting her next move. Micha grabbed one of the Dancing Pansies and did the waltz with him. Just once around the floor; then he abandoned the Dancing Pansy and walked out. Some people said he was bawling, others that he was blushing and shaking. But his waltz had been impeccable. He'd even taken the lead, so good was his dancing now.

In the mailbox, a few days later, Micha found a letter that had neither a name nor a return address but was sealed with a little red heart. Wasting no time, he ripped the letter from its envelope and proceeded out of the building, where he collided with the Designated Precinct Enforcer. The letter escaped Micha's grasp and, the day being windy, sailed away. He wanted to chase after it, but the DPE grabbed him by the collar and insisted on checking his ID. The letter simply floated away, all the way over to the death strip, where it became entangled in some bushes. Not that Micha could see this. He found out only later, by attaching a mirror to a broom handle and peering down into the death strip. Whereupon, rather than just give up, he did everything he could to get his hands on it.

It was the first love letter Micha had ever received, and it had landed in the death strip. Micha had no idea what was in it. He didn't even know if the letter was from Miriam. It might have just been Shrapnel who'd written it. Or the Dancing Pansy he'd waltzed with. Maybe the letter hadn't even been for Micha; maybe it was for his sister, Sabine. Naturally, he wished more than anything else in the world that the letter was from Miriam. In the weeks and months that followed, his entire life revolved around that letter. At all costs, he had to get his hands on it, and under no circumstances was he willing to ask Miriam about it, because he could never admit to her that her letter had flown into the death strip. It was ridiculous, an insult really, Micha thought. And if the sender wasn't Miriam and he asked her about a love letter, he would make himself no less ridiculous, for being so vain as to imagine she would write him a love letter.

Non, je ne regrette rien

First Micha tried to fish for the letter. He did this in concert with Mario. Mario held the mirror and directed Micha's fishing line to where he could see the letter. Instead of a hook, they were using an eraser dipped in Kittifix glue. All the gummed-up eraser had to do was touch the letter. Then Mario and Micha would wait a few minutes, until the Kittifix had set and the letter could be fetched over the Wall.

Mario wasn't the least bit jealous of Micha's success with Miriam. As it happened, he'd just now "stumbled on something" himself: a woman he met in an elevator on Leipziger Straße. She looked the way he'd always imagined a Parisienne: red hair cascading from under a beret, a turtleneck sweater, a book of Sartre under her arm. She was a couple of years older than Mario, in her early twenties. Yet again, Mario and Lensy were discussing which college majors were unpolitical—or rather, the fact that there *were* no nonpolitical majors. Not even medicine, since doctors were expected to make a special effort if a National People's Army officer came under the knife. When Mario and Lensy exited on the sixth floor, with a "*Ciao*" to the Sartre reader, she wished them "a nice rest of the evening." The last thing Mario saw was her promising, cryptic smile behind the closing elevator door . . .

"She smiled like Mona Lisa!" Mario said to Micha as they crouched by the Wall. Micha was so eager to hear where things had gone with Mario and the Mona Lisa of Leipziger Straße, he'd all but forgotten they were waiting for the Kittifix to dry.

Having seen her press 13, Mario raced up the stairs. As he ran, like a man on fire, he was glad he didn't have to go farther than the thirteenth floor, because Lensy had told him that the high-rise apartments on Leipziger Straße had only been built to keep the Axel Springer Tower from being visible from the East. Lensy always seemed to know stuff like that. The Springer Tower stood directly beyond the Wall, on the West side, and if Mario had been unlucky he might have had to run higher than the height of the Springer Tower. Before he could waste further thought on this, he reached the thirteenth floor and tumbled out into the hallway. At the far end, it seemed to him, a door had just closed . . . And it opened again, and the woman from the elevator was in the doorway, smiling at Mario, and again her smile was like Mona Lisa's. Mario scrambled to his feet and approached her, fully spent, gasping for breath, his vision dark.

"And what did you say to her?" asked Micha. He could picture the scene very clearly.

"I said to her: Do you know any unpolitical college majors?"

Instead of an answer, the woman from the elevator gave him yet another smile, to which Mario said, "You smile like

Mona Lisa." The woman fielded the compliment placidly. "Maybe it's because I'm a painter," she said, beckoning Mario into her apartment. It was more like a cave than an apart-ment, with big pictures on the walls and homemade fantasy lamps.

They talked the whole evening and deep into the night. What had started with Mario's random question about nonpo-litical majors became an introductory lesson in existentialism. Mario's elevator acquaintance might have smiled like Mona Lisa, but she was an existentialist through and through. No one has to do anything they don't feel like doing, the Existen-tialist said vehemently to Mario. Every person is responsible for himself, and every person is to blame for his own unhap-piness. You always have the freedom to make decisions, she said, and so you can't blame anyone else for the things you do. To Mario, this was something utterly, utterly different . . . It was all so new, so BIG. It really did have to do with freedom, with something special, with absolutely everything. That a person whose window looked out on the death strip was sing-ing a hymn to freedom, with such vehemence, was not only impressive to Mario; it was life-changing. All night long, over and over, Edith Piaf sang "Non, je ne regrette rien." We're condemned to freedom, the Existentialist said as she uncorked their third bottle of Bärenblut, whose labels she'd pasted over with handwritten Château Lafite labels. Mario asked if they were also condemned to listen to this song for-ever. Yes, the Existentialist replied, because, number one, the record player won't turn itself off, and, number two, nothing will ever stop if you don't stand up for yourself.

The Existentialist got up and looked out the window,

where the death strip was lit by arc lights. She'd drunk more than a bottle of wine. "We're condemned to freedom," she said. "And you know what that means for the Wall? Do you know what Sartre would say about the Berlin Wall?"

Since Mario wasn't yet entirely clear about existentialism, he had to guess: "That someday I'll be able to drive to the West."

"No," she said, "exactly the opposite."

"That I'll *never* be able to drive to the West?"

"That someday the Wall won't exist anymore," the Existentialist said. This was so outrageous to Mario, it was beyond imagining. He could never have formulated the thought that the Wall could just suddenly not be there. The Existentialist turned off Edith Piaf and put on "Je t'aime"—she knew what she wanted. From that point on, she spoke in whispers. "The only way to make yourself free is by making everyone else free, too," she said, beginning to free herself and Mario. "Do you get what I mean by that?" she whispered. "What Jean-Paul means by that?" Mario didn't get it, but there was a lot that he did understand. They started half an hour after midnight and didn't stop until it was nearly five—a truly existentialist number—and when Mario woke up the next morning she was sitting on the edge of the bed, naked, wearing only her beret, and laughed at Mario: "So, did I just de-boy you?"

Mario was the first of the clique from the grounds who'd been with a woman, and Micha wanted an exact account of everything. How it was done, no detail spared. Mario stood up and gave a demonstration, moving his hips the way he'd done it the night before. Micha stood up, too, and tried to imitate it. "Like this?" he asked. And they stood there facing each other, copulating to themselves, and Micha asked, "How long do you have to keep doing this?"

By the time Mario finished his story, the Kittifix had been dry for a long time. Since the events in Mario's story had occurred the night before, he was so tired that he'd mistaken a white plastic bag in the mirror for the letter. When Micha finally reeled in the line, with nothing but a plastic bag stuck to the eraser, entire school groups from the West were jeering at him: "Congrats, Zonie, you hit the jackpot! A plastic bag from your side!"

Three weeks later, Mario and Micha were summoned to Erdmute Löffeling's office. They had no idea what for. This wasn't a good sign, especially since a man they didn't know was sitting with Erdmute Löffeling. She was leafing through a magazine from the West, shaking her head and periodically sighing, emitting little moans. Mario and Micha didn't understand what their principal was doing leafing through a magazine from the West. By and by, the stranger collected himself, took a deep breath, and said, in a pained voice, "One of the disagreeable tasks that a secretary of the Party's district leadership must perform is to regularly read the enemy." He paused to give Mario and Micha time to consider the import of the words he'd spoken, and Mario duly expressed his sympathy for the Party functionary, by remarking, with a sigh, "Yes, such are the hardships of an otherwise rather excellent job." Mario said this in such a sincere tone that the secretary of the Party district leadership would never have guessed he was being made fun of. But when the Party creature handed Mario and Micha the magazine, they were dumbstruck. The problem was instantly apparent to them. When Micha looked up from the page and saw his principal's stony face, his fear of her was so intense that she assumed the twisted aspect of a monster: Erdmute Löffeling's head was much larger than Micha had realized.

It had never happened that he couldn't get out of a situation. Even as a third grader, Micha hadn't let himself be outsmarted. Erdmute Löffeling had suddenly appeared in class and written VIETNAM on the blackboard, and Micha was called to the front by his teacher. He was asked to point to a spot on the globe where there were children who had things especially bad. Micha guessed that he was facing anti-imperialist "volunteer" work, and he was already sick of collecting recyclables. So he pointed to the USA. How could Erdmute Löffeling object to that? What was she supposed to say? No, the children in the USA had things great? "Yes, but where else?" she said. "The Federal Republic of Germany," Micha said, and here again Erdmute Löffeling was thwarted. "Yes, and where else?" she asked. "Well, anywhere capitalist," Micha said. "And what about Vietnam?" Erdmute Löffeling asked the nine-year-old Micha. His answer: "Children in Vietnam are doing a lot better, because children in Vietnam are looking forward to the liberation that their invincible people are fighting for!"

What Mario and Micha saw, in the magazine that the Party creature held out to them, was a picture of the two of them stretching out their hands like beggars, beseeching the onlooker with widened eyes. Mario and Micha had been beautifully captured, and the photograph, expressive enough in itself, was adorned with a caption: *Privation in the East—how long will the people stay silent?*

The Party creature and Erdmute Löffeling said nothing, letting Micha and Mario stew under a long and punishing glare. Micha cleared his throat tentatively, and then, with sudden self-assurance, indeed almost swagger, declared, "You can see it!" He paused for dramatic effect and continued, with rising enthusiasm, "You can see how *they're* the ones who are lying. The fact that they're resorting to lies like this, it goes to show how close they are to collapsing. I'd love to see more lies like this! Because the dirtier the lies, the more driven into a corner the enemy is."

Micha knew how to get some breathing room in a certain kind of situation. The Party creature seemed very much swayed by his argument. That the boy had created bad press was less than desirable, but his analysis was intriguing: *The dirtier the lies, the more driven into a corner the enemy is.* Erdmute Löffeling disapproved of Micha's syntax, but there was no stopping him: "When the lies are at their dirtiest, the enemy is driven-est into a corner." The Party creature began to give some thought to Micha's future—someday even Karl-Eduard von Schnitzler would be retiring as the national newscaster. In the meantime, Micha was sentenced to prepare a contribution to the discussion with the mellifluous title "The Lie, the Enemy, and Class Struggle," in which he would be expected to proceed dialectically from his personal experience to a universalizing moral.

Micha had once again twisted a story to suit himself, and the Party creature, closing the magazine on the incriminating picture, had gone so far as to give Micha a friendly nod, when Mario's mouth sprang open. He said defiantly: "The hunger for freedom is more powerful than the hunger for bread! Sartre said that! Or—Mahatma Gandhi? Or was it the hunger for human rights?" Mario, in his excitement, was thoroughly confused, but he knew what he wanted: to plead guilty to everything taboo—to Sartre and Gandhi, to freedom and human rights. These five words were so taboo that he really shouldn't even have known them, let alone allowed them out of his mouth. Micha, trying to contain the damage, explained that what Mario meant, obviously, was *so-called* freedom and *so-called* human rights. It was no use. The Party creature turned to Micha and said icily, "If your so-called friend doesn't come to his so-called senses, he's going to get the so-called boot!" Mario screamed at him: "But I'm not coming to my so-called senses!"

Here an unfamiliar word came into play: *relegation*. Not even Lensy knew this word. But everyone immediately grasped what it meant. No one would have dreamed of using this word. It sounded so merciless, so cold. It sounded like a thing there was no defending yourself against.

Lensy was reluctant to say to Mario that he'd finally found a course of study that he considered absolutely nonpolitical. It was weeks before he dared ask Mario if there was anything political about oral-medicine technical school. Mario only had to think for two seconds before agreeing with Lensy: oral medicine was unpolitical. "But do you seriously want to poke around in strangers' mouths, just so you can have peace of mind?"

The Existentialist comforted Mario. Once again they listened to "Non, je ne regrette rien" the whole evening. "You know what she's singing?" the Existentialist asked. "She's singing, 'No, I don't regret anything.'" More than once, she also said, "Important people always get kicked out of school." Mario didn't believe that getting the boot made him an important person, and she didn't disagree. "But it's the start of something."

She was right about that. It was the beginning of the most beautiful time in Mario's life. He could kill the alarm clock every morning and go back to sleep, he had a girlfriend, and he had no one to tell him what he should and shouldn't do. Rules are anathema to existentialists in any case, but Mario didn't have anyone who even *tried* to tell him what he shouldn't do. He and the Existentialist became the dream couple. They did all the things that other people are forever only wishing they could do. When the weather was nice, they went swimming, and when the weather was bad they had pillow fights. They fed each other breakfast with their eyes closed. They never went to bed alone anymore, didn't even take a shower alone! And sometimes they said: This is how it must have been in Paradise. They did a lot of reading and talked about the Bible and other great religions (giving the highest marks to Buddhism), about Sigmund Freud, Friedrich Nietzsche, Leon Trotsky, and Rudolf Steiner (giving Jean-Paul Sartre the highest marks). They experimented with food by inventing new recipes and baking their own bread, and by fasting.

The Existentialist was taken with the idea of escaping to the wilds of eastern Brandenburg and alternately philosophizing and reading there. She wanted to spend a whole summer lying in a barrel, like Diogenes. Under cover of night, she rolled a barrel out through the underground supply route for the Berlin Market Hall. For the launching of her barrel residency, she chose the Whitsun holidays, to get away from the youth festival that was taking place in Berlin. When she crawled into the barrel, on the shore of Lake Stechlin, she took a large stack of books with her, all manner of philosophers and Schiller's *Wilhelm Tell*. But she lasted only four hours in the barrel, because it was too uncomfortable. "If Alexander the Great had asked me what I wanted, I wouldn't have said, 'Don't stand between me and the sun.' I would have said, 'Gimme a pillow for my ass!'"

And so Mario and the Existentialist went back to Berlin and learned what they'd missed. During the youth festival, there had been an incident that would long be discussed on the Sonnenallee.

Avanti Popolo

The Kuppisches' quartered guests, who slept on the air mattresses that Mrs. Kuppisch had borrowed from their Stasi neighbor, were two Saxons from Pirna, near Dresden: "the Olaf" and "the Udo." Without exception, they introduced every first name with a definite article. Until the Kuppisches figured this out, they thought Udo's girlfriend was named Theanna, but her name was simply Anna; Olaf and Udo always referred to her as *the Anna*. They weren't exactly the brightest bulbs. This might have been related to their coming from the Valley of the Clueless, the area where there was no reception for Western television. When the Olaf and the Udo saw that the Wall was directly outside the window, they asked if West Berlin was over there, and Mrs. Kuppisch answered, with a sigh, "Yes, unfortunately." The Olaf and the Udo were slack-jawed with amazement. Finally one of them confessed: "We couldn't do it, this life of constant danger." The other one remarked that, with all the "criminality over that way," there were bound to be stray bullets. Mrs. Kuppisch sighed again, saying, "Yes, you just have to learn to live with it." She didn't feel like setting them straight. And yet, if only she'd looked after them a little bit, there might never have been a nighttime border incident in which the Olaf and the Udo shut down all traffic to the West. Afterward, the Kuppisches were summoned to police headquarters *for clarification of a circumstance.* "You don't have to explain it to me," Mr. Kuppisch said grimly, as he read his summons. "It's the Stasi!" Mrs. Kuppisch's nerves were completely shot. "I only let them stay with us so Misha could go to the Red Monastery! There was no way I could have known . . ."

No, there was no way of knowing that the Olaf and the Udo would try to ignite a global communist revolution. They took it upon themselves to agitate among the West Berlin drivers at the Sonnenallee border crossing, supposing that the drivers would start a revolution in West Berlin out of sheer socialist enthusiasm. The Olaf and the Udo were so sure of their plan, they actually laid twenty marks on the victory of global communism in the next ten days. The only problem was that the plan had been hatched with blood-alcohol levels between point one two and point one six. Olaf and Udo had sat with their district delegation in Lichtenberg Park, boozing and arguing about politics, at first in general terms, later about the chances of victory in a global communist revolution. "If the workers could see what our life is really like . . . they'd rise up against their systematic exploitation!" cried the Olaf and the Udo. One of them slurring his words, the other one seeing double, they peeled off to the Sonnenallee border crossing, flagged down late-model Mercedes sedans, and performed what they imagined was agitation. They extolled the blessings of socialism to the Westerners.

"FREE EDUCATION!"

"FREE HEALTH CARE!"

"STABLE PRICES!"

Even to them, it seemed bizarre, and they were soon at the point of giving up. But when, to Olaf's cry of "LOW RENT," a stubborn Mercedes driver rejoined, "In tiny apartments!" the two of them resorted to more drastic action: anyone who wanted to return to the West would first be compelled to sing songs of the struggle. The Olaf sang in a bellowing voice and patiently conducted while the Udo affixed little paper flags to the Mercedes hood ornaments. By midnight, a choir of ten West Berliners was valiantly singing "Avanti Popolo" and waving flags of the Democratic Republic, but when the Olaf, following the song, began to hold forth on the Revolution, one of the West Berliners cut him off: "People, I'm all for revolution. But that vegetable store on the corner? It puts a damper on my revolutionary zeal. Yeah, I'm aware, you got your soup greens all year round. Awesome!" Not long after this, two paramedics showed up, put the Olaf and the Udo in straitjackets, and drove away.

As always, an incident had its aftermath. The Kuppisches were summoned to police headquarters *for clarification of a circumstance*. But they weren't blamed for the incident, despite having provided guest quartering for Olaf and Udo. Mrs. Kuppisch was able to keep hoping that Micha could go to the Red Monastery. But the Party functionary who'd gotten Mario kicked out of school now wanted to show "our fellow people on the Sonnenallee" that an incident like this would be met with a response. And so, all of a sudden, the vegetable store on the corner had fabulous offerings. It had occurred to the Party creature that the first thing and the last thing West Berliners saw of the GDR was a greengrocer with sorry offerings. *Soup greens all year round.* That one hurt.

There needed to be *one* vegetable store in the East like the ones in the West, and, what's more, it needed to be cheaper. The Party creature handled it all himself, investing so much energy that he barely had time to read the enemy. Within a few weeks, the ratty old vegetable store had fabulous offerings. But there had been a complete failure to anticipate what would happen then. Word very quickly spread about a fabulous produce store at the short end of the Sonnenallee. The thing took on a life of its own, since it was practically required by courtesy, if someone mentioned that she'd been shopping, to respond by asking, "And did they have anything?" In a matter of days, the vegetable store on the Sonnenallee became genuinely famous, downright legendary. The lines that formed outside it got longer and longer. Which meant that the first thing and the last thing Western visitors saw of the GDR was a very, very long line . . . No, this wasn't the way the Party creature had imagined it. He ordered the store closed immediately, and he proceeded to ponder which goods were exclusively available in the GDR. Something of that sort, he thought, needed to be sold in the little grocery. In his wildest dreams, the Party creature saw a huge line of West Berliners in front of the new store. Finally, the perfect idea came to him; but he kept it secret.

The store was renovated, its window covered with a sheet,

and no one on the Sonnenallee knew what was coming. Naturally, rumors abounded. A store selling things you couldn't
get in the West—what kind of store could that be? In the end,
the rumor that prevailed was that the store would sell only
exports: guitars, hand-carved Christmas pyramids, Wernes-
grüner beer . . .

On opening day, the Sonnenallee was swarming with
people full of hope, loaded with cash. When the store window
was finally unveiled, they saw red flags, GDR flags, portraits
of Chairman Honecker, May Day pins, Free German Youth
shirts, Young Pioneer badges and drums, in every conceivable
size and variation. That same day, seven new applications to
leave the GDR were officially filed. "Water always getting
shut off, never anything to buy but Red trash," grumbled one
of the applicants, a streetcar driver like Mr. Kuppisch.

In fact, the store did rather good business, especially in
later years, when the exchange rate was so high that Western
visitors hardly knew what to do with all the Eastern money
they were forced to buy. Many of them took their last opportunity to dump their money by purchasing paper flags
and other curiosities. The vegetable lady did a nice job with
it: "For three-twenny, I can give you another hunnert little
flags. Nope, an FGY shirt like that one costs eight-fitty, but
if you're a little short you can make it up in Western." She
held on to the Western money, replenishing the cash register
from her wallet. The dribs and drabs amounted to ten Western every day, which over the months added up to a tidy an-
nual sum. The vegetable lady became the grande dame of the
Sonnenallee, smelling of Paris, decked out like the Queen of
the Night, her shoulders draped with shimmering silk shawls.

She knew she was a good catch; whoever married her would be able to buy imported Black and Decker tools at the Intershop. She still had the figure of a grocery monger, still sold paper flags and pictures of Honecker, but she stood in her store as if she were selling jewelry at the toniest of addresses. And the weirdest thing about it: even though the shop was full of flags and badges and Young Pioneer scarves, the people at the short end of the Sonnenallee continued to call it the vegetable store, and she remained the vegetable lady.

Mr. Kuppisch today likes to say, "That time in the East was one crazy kind of Schüetzenfest—every shot they took blew up in their face." To explain what he means, he tells the story of the vegetable store on the Sonnenallee. Once upon a time, the Kuppisches quartered a pair of guests from Saxony, to make sure that Micha got into the Red Monastery.

The heart a bit larger

When the Kuppisches were summoned to police headquarters *for clarification of a circumstance*, Micha was the last one allowed to leave. It was his first arrest (although he hadn't actually been arrested). Leaving the Baumschulenweg S-Bahn station, heading toward the Sonnenallee, he very much hoped he might run into Miriam, but this time, alas, he didn't. Micha often walked this way with Miriam, down Baumschulenstraße to the Sonnenallee. He always intended to walk slowly, so as to have more time with her, but he was invariably so excited, so buoyant, that a leisurely side-by-side stroll remained only a notion. He wished that, just once, he might get stopped and frisked in Miriam's presence, as evidence that he tended toward the wrong side of the law. But the DPE was notably lenient whenever Miriam was with Micha. On the plus side, it also never happened that the AWO drove up alongside Miriam and stole her away from him. When they reached the spot where Baumschulenstraße meets the Sonnenallee, Miriam and Micha parted; he went to the side of the street with even-numbered addresses, she to the side with odd-numbered ones.

In none of these chance meetings was Micha able to ascertain whether the love letter, still lying in the death strip, was from Miriam. He couldn't think of any way of finding out without making himself look ridiculous. Not that he wasn't still hoping for the promised kiss. He was waiting the way a farmer waits for rain. One evening, when their paths crossed again on the way home, Micha thought the moment might finally have arrived. It was the last day of school, the start of the long vacation, and everyone was leaving town. Micha to the Baltic, Miriam to the High Tatra Mountains. Miriam had to laugh—the year before, she'd gone to the Baltic and Micha to the High Tatras. It was a lovely warm summer night, the air soft, everything peaceful, and when they reached the spot where their paths divided, Miriam again didn't seem to be thinking about it. "You once promised me something," Micha complained. "Yes," she said calmly, "but what I said was: someday." Micha swallowed hard and gave a cry of despair: "I could be waiting forever!" "So what?" Miriam said, as softly as a lamb. "It just means you'll always have something to look forward to. If you know I'm going to kiss you someday, you'll never have to be sad."

And home she went. All summer long, Micha considered the sentence that Miriam had spoken, and he concluded that he'd underestimated her. Had assumed, like everyone else, that she was naïve, simply because she was staggeringly beautiful. *If you know I'm going to kiss you someday, you'll never have to be sad.* A person who can say such a thing knows something about waiting, about yearning, about hoping—in other words, the things we spend most of our lives doing. Micha saw that if he wanted to have a role in Miriam's life he needed to grow up. He recalled that he'd never felt more mature, more manly and adult, than at the dance-school graduation ball. It suddenly seemed childish to have imagined that having his ID checked by the DPE would increase his prestige, or to have insisted on the promised kiss. Or to pretend to be someone he wasn't. To get the kiss that Miriam had promised him, Micha needed to become an *adult*. He didn't know what this might entail, he only knew that it wouldn't be easy, and that it wouldn't happen overnight. But it was just as Miriam had said: He would always have something to look forward to. And he looked forward to it.

The bottom-dog Russian boot cleaner of the Eastern Steppe

One day, when Heinz was again coming to the East, the border guard took him aside and showed him the white stripe that marked the border. The stripe had just been repainted, and the guard confided to Heinz, in a whisper, that the new stripe ran ten centimeters farther to the west. He'd already done the math: the stripe only had to be repainted once every two years, and moved a mere ten centimeters farther to the west each time, for Eastern Europe to reach the Atlantic coast in seventy million years, "and if we repaint the stripe *every* year, we'll get the job done in half that time." Heinz, at a loss for words, remained at a loss when the guard said rousingly, "Don't you worry, we'll get you liberated."

* * *

We didn't have passports. Within the Eastern bloc, we had to show border officials our national ID booklet and a slip of paper known as a "travel permit for visa-free tourist travel."

Most people got their permit, but not everyone. The Existentialist was caught at the Leipzig Book Fair stealing a tiny paperback volume of essays by Simone de Beauvoir, and this was apparently enough for her to be denied travel privileges the following summer. The stupidity was especially hard on Mario, who'd gone to the trouble of cutting his hair, after hearing that longhairs weren't even allowed into the Eastern bloc. He got his travel permit, but she didn't. Insult to injury, he was hairstyle-wise again the lowest of the low.

* * *

For a while, Sabine's latest was a mountain climber. His name was Lutz. Lutz had his own method of crossing borders without waiting seventy million years, or even just half that. While Lutz and Sabine packed their backpacks for a trip to Siberia, all the other Kuppisches, including Uncle Heinz, were treated to a lecture from Lutz on the art of exotic travel without a passport. Mr. Kuppisch didn't think the two of them would even make it into the Soviet Union, let alone Siberia—the only way to get there was with a *grupa*, an organized tour group. To the Russians, the very phrase *individual tourism* was an absurdity. "You can file as many petitions as you like!"

Lutz rolled his eyes conspiratorially and said just two words, but he spoke them like a magician casting a spell: "Transit visa." Pausing for dramatic effect, he explained: "And then, once you're in, you stay in."

Heinz proudly waved his passport. "I can move around freely with this, a free person, anywhere in the Free World."

Lutz snorted contemptuously; he considered passports pe-
tit bourgeois. Sabine proceeded to gush that Lutz had actually
been to Mongolia—and to China! Mrs. Kuppisch, normally
the paragon of caution, thought this was very interesting and
wanted it all explained to her in detail. Lutz was delighted to
finally be able to lay out the particulars of his system: whenever he went on a trip, he brought along every form of identification ever issued to him, counting on the border guards to
assume, from the plethora of IDs, that everything must be in
order. In addition to his national ID booklet, he brought his
social-security booklet (into which he'd pasted a small photo
of himself, so that it looked like a passport) and his military
pass, where he'd been photographed in uniform, to state-
sanctioned effect. He even brought his old Young Pioneers ID
card. If, after presenting his national ID, his social-security
booklet, and his military pass, he still wasn't allowed to cross
a border, he would pull out his Young Pioneers card with a
magnificent, expansive gesture: "Oh, *that's* what you're looking for—how great I have it with me!"

"And you got all the way to Mongolia like that?" Mrs.
Kuppisch asked.

"No," said Lutz, "to go to Mongolia you need an invitation." The invitation was something you could write yourself, Lutz said, but to make his self-composed invitation look
official he'd put a Mongolian coin underneath it and, with a
pencil, shaded the national emblem of Mongolia onto it, to
create an official seal. An "officially certified invitation" was
required, and wherever there's an office, Lutz thought, there's
a seal. He'd fished the coin, a five-tugrik piece, out of the
Neptune Fountain, into which tourists from around the world

threw change. Every week, for two months, Lutz drove to the Neptune Fountain, stood ankle-deep in water, and hunted for rare coins, until finally a Mongol tossed five tugriks into the fountain. Self-composed invitation in hand, Lutz went to the agency. No one there was familiar with the official seal of Mongolia, and so Lutz got his papers. The following year, a friend of his decided he wanted to go to Mongolia, too. Thanks to an acquaintance Lutz had made on his vacation, a genuine invitation with a genuine official seal, from a genuine Mongolian government office, was forthcoming.

"That is so excellent," Sabine said. "Whenever one of us feels like going to Mongolia, we'll have our own Mongolian connection!"

"Nope," Lutz said. "Won't work."

When Lutz's friend had gone to pick up his papers at the agency, he was denied his documents because the official seal was incorrect. "You need the other seal to get an invitation," they said. When they showed him the correct seal, Lutz's friend's jaw dropped: it was Lutz's letter of invitation from the previous year.

"And I don't have a five-tugrik coin anymore," Lutz said. "So we can scratch Mongolia off the list."

Mrs. Kuppisch was also curious how Lutz had gotten into China. "China was really hard," Lutz said. In the course of half a day spent watching the Soviet-China border station, his eye was caught by a soldier who he presumed was the bottom dog because he was cleaning everyone else's boots, fifty pairs of Russian army boots, outside the border barracks. Apart from that, nothing was happening out there on the Eastern Steppe, maybe one car passing every couple of hours. Lutz waited until the bottom dog was given charge of the passport control point. Needless to say, Lutz's documents were less than complete, and the bottom dog, after lengthy indecisive leafing, refused to let Lutz through. Whereupon Lutz made such an operatic scene that the bottom dog's superior got involved—and, of course, reached the opposite conclusion, because by definition everything a bottom dog does is wrong. When Lutz left the border station, heading into China, the bottom dog had been sent to scrub the latrines.

Mrs. Kuppisch still wasn't done. She wanted to know how Lutz would work things if he wanted to cross the border right outside their door. "No chance," Lutz said. "Ab-so-lute-ly none." This Wall could make a person sad and despairing. Especially when the idea of crossing it was dismissed by a person who'd been all the way to Mongolia and China.

* * *

Mrs. Kuppisch, however, believed there *was* a chance—her chance. Mrs. Kuppisch was the one who'd found Helene Rumpel's passport, and she'd been working on herself ever since. She wanted to look like the passport's owner, Helene Rumpel. And then, as Helene Rumpel, she wanted to pass through the barricades. Helene Rumpel was twenty years older than Mrs. Kuppisch—a problem she'd solved at her little dressing table. Mrs. Kuppisch had clothes and shoes from the West, and in her purse were an open packet of Kukident denture cleaner and an unused West Berlin rail ticket. She could sign Helene Rumpel's name as well as she could sign her own. One evening, when the light was poor, she set out to pass through the checkpoint as Helene Rumpel. Anxious as always, she stopped to observe the border crossing from a safe distance. She spotted a young couple on their way back to West Berlin, and when she saw how relaxed and self-assured they were, how loudly they talked, how artificially they laughed, how much space they took up—when she saw all this, she knew that it took more than just a passport, shoes, clothes, and Kukident to make her a Westerner. What's more, she knew that she could never be like them. That she really did have no chance of crossing the border right outside her door.

Mrs. Kuppisch went back home. What else could she do? She didn't feel ashamed of her anxiety, which had prevented her from traversing those last thirty meters; she'd already suspected that she didn't belong to the hard-nosed half of humanity. But now, with no reason to make herself older, she became her former self again. Back in the apartment, she went straight to her dressing table. When Mr. Kuppisch came home, he couldn't believe his eyes. Mrs. Kuppisch seemed even younger than she had before—so, at least, said everyone who saw her in the first weeks of her rejuvenation. No one knew how to explain it. Micha speculated that she had a secret lover, Sabine that she had a new hairdresser, while Heinz saw an indication of lung cancer, it being a well-known fact that cancer patients become optimistic as the end approaches.

Je t'aime

The Existentialist, who wasn't allowed to leave the country because she'd been caught stealing Simone de Beauvoir at the Leipzig Book Fair, went to the Baltic with Mario. There, an asthmatic from Sandersdorf showed them a medicament suitable for drug experiments. Mario and the Existentialist called it Saxon Locoweed. You could get it at the drugstore. The trick was to mix it with cola and swallow it in one gulp. The Sandersdorf asthmatic also talked about a chemical factory in Sandersdorf that turned the morning fog yellow. Mario and the Existentialist were massively excited: a drug that made the morning fog look yellow was exactly the drug they wanted to take.

When Mario and the Existentialist returned to Leipziger Straße, they hazarded an experiment with Saxon Locoweed. The effect exceeded their wildest expectations. "I'm in Mudsville!" Mario shouted, besotted. The Existentialist smiled dreamily and hummed children's songs, which she called *kiddren songs*. It lasted exactly two hours. Then came the time of suffering. They were utterly dry-mouthed. They needed to drink, but the refrigerator was empty. And today, of all days, the water had been shut off again. They ought to have noticed it when the toilet tank didn't refill after flushing. Their thirst became ever more terrible. On top of that, they went blind— just for a couple of hours, but it prevented them from going shopping. The only water they could find in their apartment was a little mouthful in the sink trap. "This is disgusting, but it tastes delicious," the Existentialist said.

They were both still blind when Micha came by and rang the doorbell. It was about the love letter again; the thing gave him no rest. He wanted to dig under the Wall with a toy tin shovel—just enough to get his arm through. He needed their help, he needed them to be his lookouts. "We're blind!" Mario said. "How are we supposed to be your lookouts?" When Micha looked at their eyes, he was frightened: all he could see was pupil; their eyes had no irises.

"The drug has turned you into monsters!" he wailed.

The Existentialist was understandably curious about the letter in question, and as Micha proceeded to tell the full story of Miriam he felt like a perplexed man confiding in a wise blind woman. The Existentialist had the idea of throwing a party some time when Mario had the run of his parents' apartment. All Micha would have to do was wait until "Je t'aime" was playing and then look deep into Miriam's eyes. "The rest is so easy, we don't even have to talk about it."

The idea was horribly upsetting to Micha. "She is something very special, I mean, this is not the kind of thing you just go out and get, and it is definitely not happening at the push of a button like everybody else! There's something about her that's so—*mysterious*. When I'm reading a book, I'm thinking about her, when I listen to a song, I'm thinking about her . . ."

"Micha, 'Je t'aime' always helps," Mario said, speaking from experience. The Existentialist trained her blind eyes on nothing and said, beaming, "Yes, I see it so clearly."

If Mario and Micha had imagined the fiasco the Existentialist's idea would lead to, they would never, ever have planned a party. Afterward, no one could say whom it had been worse for; some people said what happened at the party was worse for Mario, others that the party had been singularly catastrophic for Micha. But beforehand, of course, no one could foresee that the party would end in utter debacle, and so it turned into a huge thing, possibly the biggest party ever thrown at the short end of the Sonnenallee. Among the guests, besides Micha and Mario and the Existentialist, were not only Lensy and Fatty and Frizz but Sabine, who'd again replaced her latest. The new latest was a student of theology, an attractive choice in those days. The Dancing Pansies from the dance school had come, and Frizz had tracked down the tattooed Stones fan Frankie, the unlucky Bergmann, the record dealer Edge, even the Strausberg hippie. The Existentialist had invited the entire avant-garde scene. Shrapnel was there, even the Sandersdorf asthmatic was there. Mario wasn't prepared for this. The more people who showed up, the more he feared for the safety of the antique musical instruments, dating from across four centuries, that were hanging and standing and lying all over the apartment. Mario's father had been collecting old instruments since his confirmation. By and by, the Strausberg hippie took a seventeenth-century mandolin off the wall and, pronouncing it "in urgent need of blues tuning," set about retuning the instrument.

Mario didn't notice, because he and his existentialist girlfriend and the Dancing Pansies were in the kitchen, discussing the possibility of establishing an autonomous anti-republic inside the GDR. "Everyone could buy two thousand square meters of land!" said one of Pansies. All they needed to do, the Existentialist said, was quietly get a large number of people to buy up land and then band together as a renegade territory . . . She was very excited about the idea, but Mario had no faith in it, and so the discussion became heated: "Existentialism is a get-your-head-out-of-your-ass philosophy, not an it-probably-won't-work-so-I'd-rather-not-be-bothered philosophy!"

Even Sabine needed something explained to her that night. When she took a glass of wine from Johannes, her theologian, and thanked him with a friendly "Amen," he enlightened her about something he'd been meaning to tell her for some time—that *amen* didn't mean "thank you" and *hallelujah* didn't mean "hello." Behind them, a game of skat was being played, the cards literally drummed down: Edge and Frankie and Fatty, lacking a table, had crowded around an antique kettledrum and were using it as a playing surface. You could hear how heavy the tricks were. Only Mario didn't hear them, because he was now on fire with the land-purchase idea. "Everyone has to know about it," he shouted, bursting with enthusiasm, "but it still has to be a secret!" No one asked him how he planned to manage this.

Fatty was getting off on the blues, rhyming a running commentary on the party and singing it to the tune of "Little

Red Rooster," accompanied by the Strausberg hippie's E and A and G chords on the seventeenth-century mandolin.

> *Empties flying off the balcony*
> *Smashing in the street*
> *Gonna be a reckoning—*
> *The neighbors called the heat . . .*

The neighbors did not, in fact, call the heat, but it rhymed with *street*, and there certainly were bottles flying off the balcony.

All the while, Micha anxiously paced back and forth between rooms, making everyone nervous. Miriam hadn't shown up. Might she still come? Or, after all, maybe not? Aware of what he was going through, people kept pouring things for him. "Have a drink, it'll help!" or "Have a drink, it'll take the edge off!" or "Have a drink, you'll feel better!" or "Relax, have a drink!" This was how Micha ended up drunk sooner than any of the others, and for the first time in his life. His agitation slowly abated, even as Miriam failed to appear.

Later in the evening, one of the Existentialist's friends staged a happening on the balcony: he unwrapped a buttercream cake, unzipped his pants, and pissed on the cake. Frizz came into the kitchen extremely disgusted, interrupting the land-purchase conversation, but the Existentialist reassured him: "Dude, that's the art scene, the *underground*, it takes some getting used to. Last year he started repeating everything I said back at me, word for word. Which, hey, it gets you thinking. You start being aware of what you're saying. And that's art!" There ensued a discussion of art. Frankie bared a forearm with a mermaid tattoo and said huskily, "That is art. Had it for three years and eight months!" Out on the balcony, there were shrieks of disgust. The theologian came into the kitchen, his face pale. The *customer*, as he referred to the underground artist, had up and polished off the pee-drenched cake. Even the Existentialist shuddered with revulsion, calling the artist a "filthy old pig," at which point Frizz, of all people, came to his defense: "No, that's art! When a person does something nobody else would do, it shakes things up. It's like electricity! That is electric art!"

The conversation and the blues, the clinking of bottles and the drumbeats of the skat players, gave a lively sound to the party, and Miriam was hardly noticed when she finally arrived. Sadly, the room being dark, a Bulgarian shepherd's flute from circa 1910, which the Strausberg hippie had left on the sofa within easy reach, suffered injury when Miriam sat down beside Shrapnel. "Man," the Strausberg hippie was saying, "if the fourth string breaks, too, that's it for the music." He cast a covetous glance at the shawm, but the instrument was already spoken for: Edge had pinned it between his legs and was using it as an ashtray. For quite a while now, Shrapnel had been making out with Lensy. She'd taken off his glasses and said, "You look really cute without your glasses," to which Lensy replied, "Without my glasses, you look cute to me, too." Miriam was enjoying herself, watching the two of them unashamedly. When Micha suddenly loomed up in front of her, she reacted as if he were the personification of horror.

In the moment, all Micha could do was flee. As he ran for the kitchen, in a panic, he caught his shirt on a door handle and ripped the sleeve. In the kitchen, he tore off the sleeve at the shoulder and splattered himself with beet juice, right down the front of his pants. Since Mrs. Kuppisch had long plagued him with warnings that beet stains don't come out, he applied himself to the stain with a rag and lots of water. By the time he'd finished, the wet stain on the front of his pants was no longer red. On the minus side, it was now very large. This was the moment when "Je t'aime" came on in the living room.

Mario had returned to the living room for the first time in an hour, and when he saw the chaos of antique instruments from across four centuries he demanded an explanation from Frizz, who was attempting to play a nineteenth-century bandonion with the blues band. Frizz apologized—they'd only started playing because the tape-recorder batteries were failing. "See?" Frizz said, pushing the Play button. And "Je t'aime" started up. The batteries really were dying, and the tape dragged horribly. Music always sounds horrible when it drags, but a dragging "Je t'aime," with its rolling, drowning organ, is easily twice as horrible as any other dragging music. But Mario still wanted to hear it, as a consolation, because "Je t'aime" was the song to which the Existentialist had undressed herself and him.

Micha, in the kitchen, had no way of knowing this. For him, "Je t'aime" was the signal. He was so drunk that he'd lost his misgivings about whether someone as extraordinarily special as Miriam could be brought around with the help of "Je t'aime." He lurched into the living room and positioned himself unsteadily in front of Miriam. She barely noticed his torn shirt, she was so fascinated by the large wet stain on the front of his pants. The music was dragging, and Micha was plastered. As in a nightmare, he kneeled in front of her and slurringly said, "Miriam, I know this might not be the best time, 'cause I've got this zit here, but a promise is a promise . . ." And then Micha really did try to kiss Miriam. She broke free of him, stood up, and ran away. Micha had drunk way too much to follow her. He lay down to sleep in a corner. For a pillow, he used a bagpipe from the early eighteenth century, which he inflated after knotting up all the openings. He was lying there when Mario's father returned in the morning, before the party had properly ended. The Strausberg hippie still had the mandolin in the crook of his arm and was playing the blues. One look at him, and Mario's father understood that he'd become, overnight, a collector of *broken* antique instruments from across four centuries. Everything went very quickly after that. The Strausberg hippie was forced to stop in the middle of a verse, Micha was roused, and Mario was thrown out of his parents' house.

Subversion: this way, that way, or a third way

Mario and the Existentialist loved the idea of mobilizing an underground movement to secretly buy up land, which could then be consolidated as an autonomous territory and jettisoned from the GDR. They devoted entire days and nights to drafting a constitution for the renegade region. They were of like mind regarding nonalignment, abolition of the military draft, and freedom of the press, but not about the form of government: she favored a council-style republic, he a parliamentary democracy. On weekends, they rode Mario's moped out into the country, which seemed endlessly large to them. But this was only because their moped was so slow. One day, the Existentialist said, "Mario, we should try to theoretically calculate how many people we need in the secret movement if we want to buy the whole GDR." Not counting the "firing ranges" (as the Existentialist referred to the restricted military areas, which couldn't be sold), the GDR had a hundred thousand square kilometers, give or take. She wanted Mario to do the math, but he was too lazy.

"What's the point of getting kicked out of school if I still have to do math?"

"Well, I'm a painter," she said, "so you can't expect me to do math, either." But since Mario clearly had no intention of doing it, she gave it a try. It was a gorgeous summer day, and they were lazing in a meadow.

"A kilometer is a thousand meters, right?" She tickled Mario's nose with a splendid dandelion. "So two thousand meters would be the same as two kilometers?"

Mario made a vaguely affirmative noise. And so the Existentialist calculated that if everyone could manage to buy two thousand square meters, which was two square kilometers, it followed that fifty thousand land buyers could purchase the entire GDR, except for the firing ranges. She thought this was sensational. "Mario, we'll buy the country right out from under their ass! Best to do it before the next Party congress. They'll be so busy with their theatrics, they won't even notice until it's too late."

Money for the land buy wasn't the problem. Land wasn't expensive. A square meter only cost a couple of marks. The Existentialist could paint and sell a few more pictures and also, if it came to that, knock out some costume jewelry. Mario planned to manufacture moccasins and sell them for twenty-five marks a pair. Under no circumstances would the Existentialist accept official commissions from the government. Not that it wouldn't be nice if the state financed its own demise, "but no way will I paint their pictures."

Although it was true that, as she said, the higher-ups would be too busy with their theatrics before the Party congress to notice anything, it was not the case that the theatrics were confined to the period before Party congresses. We staggered through the campaigns, and there was always something. No sooner had we heaved a sigh of relief, at the conclusion of a Party congress, than an anniversary appeared on the horizon, attended by a new campaign. After the anniversary had been survived, the newspapers opined that it might be a good time to vote again, in order to ratify the Party's policy successes. In other words, another campaign. And no sooner were the elections behind us than the Party determined that, in view of this tremendous vote of confidence, another congress ought to be convened.

Micha's father was of the opinion that, if there was ever a time when petitions received a positive response, it was before elections. His theory was that nothing upset the authorities more than a nonvoter, and that a snarled threat of "Yeah? Then I ain't gonna vote!" could work wonders. Anyone with half a brain took for granted that election results were artificially sweetened, but what if someone wanted sweet results without the sweetener? Once the number of yes votes had gone as high as it could go—no one cared about the difference between 99.28 and 99.55 percent—new heights of loyalty were devised, such as *going to vote in solidarity with one's collective* or *going to vote before noon* or *wearing an FGY shirt to the polls.*

Nevertheless, the elections were not without embarrassments, and the biggest of these, the total countrywide and international embarrassment, was the work of Micha's brother, Bernd. He did it while he was in the army, no less. He had a commander who was not only exceptionally zealous but so full of himself that he'd taken the code name *Everest* for radio communications. Bernd's army buddy Thomas alternately addressed Everest as "Müggelberg" and "Stalin Peak" on the radio, which in time earned the commander the nickname Müggelberg Peak. Chagrined to be named after a little sledding slope in the Berlin flatlands, Müggelberg Peak took Thomas to heart in his own way: he didn't give him a minute's rest. Thomas spent so much time on KP, he dreamed of mop buckets and floor-polishing contraptions.

On Election Sunday, Müggelberg Peak was the duty officer, the boss of the barracks, and at morning roll call the regimental commander read the Order of the Day: "Every single vote for the candidates of the National Front!" Müggelberg Peak was like a dog standing on its hind legs and begging: "At your command, Comrade Lieutenant Colonel—*every* vote!" And because Müggelberg Peak was an exceptionally zealous sort, he made the companies assemble in a long line after roll call. Then he marched down the line and gave everyone a ballot. His adjutant followed him with the ballot box. Every soldier was expected to fold the ballot once and drop it in the box. Because the dropping-in took a hair longer than the handing-out, Müggelberg Peak soon had a small lead on the adjutant.

When Müggelberg Peak reached Bernd, the adjutant had just arrived at Thomas—who refused to put his ballot in the box. Thomas choked out the words "election law" and "voting booth." Müggelberg Peak, who'd handed Bernd a ballot, went back to Thomas and roared: "The hell, refuse an order? Order of the Day, you deaf? Attention and shut up! Fold the ballot! Put it in! How about like *this* . . . Where was I?"

Bernd waved his hand. Müggelberg Peak returned to him and gave him a *second* ballot. Bernd stealthily placed it on top of the first one, folded the two of them together, and dropped them in the box without the adjutant noticing anything. Müggelberg Peak was able to report that the soldiers in his barracks had cast their votes unanimously, before nine a.m., in full dress. This was unparalleled. But then, at the public counting of the ballots, in which the soldiers all had to take part, it came to light that 578 voters had cast 579 yes votes. Thinking the adjutant had simply miscounted, Müggelberg Peak ordered a recount—the result was the same. A second recount followed, with the ballots put in piles of ten—there were still 579 votes. Müggelberg Peak tallied up the voters on the list: 578. He was starting to get mad. Müggelberg Peak wanted to be the first head of a polling station to report his results—wanted to report his hundred-percent results by 6:03 p.m. at the latest. But it wasn't so easy. Over and over, and ever more desperately, Müggelberg Peak counted the ballots. He finally went so far as to order the counting done by a recruit who was going to study math after his military service. The official announcement of the election results was delayed for hours, because one of the twenty-two thousand polling stations had failed to report its results. At this one polling station, there was one single ballot too many. Shortly before midnight, a Party creature showed up at the barracks and raged: 578 voters could only have cast 578 ballots, the 579th vote was irrelevant. Yes, Müggelberg Peak said, we thought of that ourselves, but it means that 578 voters cast 578 yes votes and one invalid vote. The Party creature continued to rage. To explain the concept of an irrelevant vote to Müggelberg Peak, he seized on a ballot that was different from all the others, the ballot cast by Thomas, who, as a supreme act of defiance, had folded it not once but twice: "Irrelevant means: makes no difference!"

Müggelberg Peak was compelled to report to the authorities that his 578 voters had cast 578 ballots with 578 votes for the National Front. This was greeted with relief at the central election office. The official results could finally be announced. The following day, there were rumors that the lateness of the announcement was evidence of electoral fraud. According to other rumors, the telephone lines had gotten so bad that not even important election results could be phoned in to Berlin. Meanwhile the Western press speculated that some kind of intra-Party opposition had delayed the count to make the election organizers look like circus animals. And it was all the fault of Müggelberg Peak. He was sentenced to give a self-critical lecture at the next Party congress. This would be a year and a half later, shortly before Bernd and Thomas and the others were discharged. Bernd said, "I never thought I'd look forward to a Party congress!"

It was one of the last normal sentences he spoke. From then on, he became more and more incomprehensible—though he was unquestionably speaking German. One night, shortly before Bernd's discharge, Mrs. Kuppisch asked him, "So, Bernd, tell us a little bit about the army. We really have no idea what it's like."

Bernd was chewing and smacking his lips and gulping down his food while he spoke. The whole family listened spellbound, but they didn't recognize him. They couldn't understand a single word. At first, they thought it was because he was talking with his mouth full, but the longer he spoke, the clearer it became that he'd picked up a whole other language in the army. "Cherries gotta ruck up," he began. "Lip off, first shirt'll make you drop twenty. We're hatting up, big evolution, company-grade Whiskey Charlie, we're black on go-juice and the unit's only thinking rack ops, and then some burn-bag second Louie hauls out the MGMs over chow. Not an issue for your two-digit midget, but your cherry's gotta stay frosty. First shirt says hands out of the pants bunkers, and it's GOFO time if you don't want a smoking—three wake-ups at the bag-nasty station. If it gets to six, he says, we'll give it a fix. Nobody's getting sprung before spring, which POs the brass. I had a ninety-six coming, and some backhoe at Central cuts me down to a seventy-two. You know how long that lug nut's gonna be pushing an ink stick?"

The Kuppisches were petrified, listening to him. "What has the army done to you, Bernd?" Mrs. Kuppisch asked, near tears. Bernd, brushing it off, said only one more thing: "Thousands came before us, millions will come after us."

No way. Mario and the Existentialist didn't believe it would keep going forever. They were working full-steam on their project of "buying the country out from under their ass." On a wall in the Existentialist's apartment was a big map where they stood and considered how best to implement their plan. There were three possible tactics: advance, constrict, or perforate. Advancing meant purchasing land in a kind of frontal movement. Whether it started in the east, the west, the north, or the south didn't matter. It would be difficult to organize but highly effective, because you could tell very quickly if you were living in a liberated area. The constriction tactic involved buying land in a variety of places and encircling the old territories. This was even harder to organize than advancing, but it was less conspicuous. "Man, if we start in the south and get to the fifty-first parallel," the Existentialist said, studying the map with Mario, "they'll see what we're up to and stop selling land farther north—and then what do we do?"

"Then Germany's divided in four," Mario said. "There'd be the East, the West, West Berlin, and us."

"That's why I'm for constriction."

"No," Mario said. "It would take too much coordination. We'd have to call our people and let them know exactly when and where they should buy. How are we supposed to do that if nobody has a phone?"

The alternative was perforation: buying land at random. At some point, the various territories would all belong to the people of the underground movement.

If their plan was exposed, they'd be facing a trial for high treason. Up until now, they hadn't known that high treason was even on the books. "High treason?" cried the Existentialist. "Can't you say it some other way? It makes me feel like Dreyfus!"

Both of them knew it would be curtains if a spy got wind of their plans. Mario kept saying, "We have to tell everybody, but it has to stay absolutely secret." Whenever Micha heard Mario say this, he couldn't help thinking of the mantra of Sabine's stagehand, who'd postulated an ironclad rule regarding cultural programs of every sort: "The better you hide the critique, the more critical you can be." At the time, the stagehand was working up a juggling act. All the while Micha was talking to him, the stagehand kept three balls in the air.

"But that means," Micha said, "the more criticisms you have, the less you can let them show!"

"Yeah, so?" replied the stagehand, his eyes on the balls.

"You're saying, if you're criticizing everything, you don't want any of it to show?"

"Exactly," the stagehand said. "If I'm criticizing everything, I'm not allowed to let any of it show."

"But that's absurd! Then nothing's ever going to change!"

"I couldn't agree more."

"No," Micha said. "If you have a fundamental critique, you've got to say it out loud!"

"And then you'll be arrested, and everyone will think you're a lunatic for having said it out loud. Which means your fundamental critique is nothing more than a lunatic's fantasy—and that's why nothing's ever going to change."

Micha needed a moment to follow the logic. The stagehand had been juggling thoughts for far longer than he'd been juggling balls. Since Micha was too baffled to speak, the stagehand launched into a different explanation, still without letting a ball drop. "You haven't figured out why nothing ever changes here? If you actually *say* what's happening, you'll be arrested, and everyone will think you're an idiot, because you didn't even know what you're not allowed to say. If you don't want to be arrested, you have to shut up about what's happening. But if you shut *up* about what's happening, nothing will ever change, because everyone will keep thinking that all's right with the world. And that is why nothing here can ever change." While Micha went off by himself to locate the flaw in this logic—he was sure that somewhere there had to be a flaw—the stagehand stayed behind, tirelessly juggling.

How Germany failed to be divided in four

Then Mario really did get arrested. No one knew exactly what happened, because Mario hadn't come back from a trip. One Saturday morning, he and the Existentialist had set out to continue their survey of the territories where land needed to be bought. Mario traveled southwest, the Existentialist northeast. By splitting up, they could survey twice as much salable land in the same amount of time. The Existentialist was arrested, too, but only when she was back in Berlin. She was told that she "might as well say" where Mario had gone and what his plans were. "We know everything anyway, and it will be easier for you later." She pretended to be completely clueless. There was no hiding how strung out she was, but she still had the presence of mind to play the jealous woman, only now putting it together that Mario had a secret girlfriend. Everyone assumed that Mario had been caught trying to flee the country—everyone but the Existentialist, who was sure that Mario would have told her. The two of them trusted each other absolutely.

When Mario was released, four days later, he explained what had happened.

The night before his arrest, he'd gone to bed late. He had to get up early the next morning, so as not to miss his train; he had more ground to cover than he could manage with his moped. On the train, he fell asleep. He didn't wake up until the train reached the end of the line. Which was the border zone. Mario hadn't meant to go this far, but now he was in the border zone. The first thing he did was check the train schedule for the next train back. A pair of transit cops patrolling the station put the eyeball on Mario immediately. In their basic training, their advanced training, and their many upper-level courses and discussion groups and on-the-job tutorials, they'd been taught to recognize a flight risk. For example, if a young man traveling in the border zone gets off a train by himself, and the first thing he does is pretend to check the train schedule, it's a textbook case of flight risk. Wearing sneakers, no less: shoes for running, for running away.

The two transit cops asked Mario for his ID. He gave them his ID. Then they wanted to see his return ticket. Mario hadn't bought one yet. O ho! they thought. Coming to the border zone without a return ticket—is this guy making it easy for us, or what?

Mario said he hadn't meant to go this far—he'd actually meant to get out at the previous stop. Aha! said the transit cops. And what was the purpose of his trip? Obviously, Mario couldn't tell them, not without blowing up the whole land-purchase plan and getting himself tried for high treason. "Done your service?" asked one of the cops, and Mario shook his head. He was trembling with fear. He knew how the transit cops would connect the dots: he's trying to avoid military service by fleeing to the West. The cops radioed Mario's name on their walkie-talkies.

"If you've ever been caught doing something at the border, now's the time to tell us."

Mario admitted that he'd been kicked out of school for posing as a starving man for Western tour buses. One of the transit cops couldn't believe it: Posing as a starving man for Western tour buses? Kicked out of school for *that*? The cop was convinced that the best thing to do was give the idiot his ID back, take him to the ticket window, and put him on the next train. The other cop, though still suspicious, agreed. Mario heaved a sigh of relief. His minutes of terror had soaked his shirt with sweat. But then, as the cop was returning the ID booklet to Mario, he noticed that Mario had slipped something into its back sleeve: the registration card for a Dutch-language course at the community college.

One of the many little oddities of the short end of the Sonnenallee was its residents' excessive interest in language courses, especially for languages spoken in countries where they couldn't travel. Perhaps it was a way to express their longing for foreign lands. Or a kind of spite: *because* we're not allowed to go there, we'll learn the language. Self-respecting parents let it be known that their children would be getting a bilingual education. English classes at the community college were always full, as were classes in French, Spanish, Portuguese, Swedish, Italian, Arabic, Sanskrit, and Hebrew. When the border with Poland was closed, people started studying Polish, and after *Sputnik* magazine was banned there was a surge in the popularity of Russian. The Existentialist studied

French; Miriam once signed up for Spanish. Her little brother wanted to study an American Indian language. But even that class was full.

It wasn't only about learning languages, it was about having contact with all the people living in places where we weren't allowed to travel. Fatty's most sought-after partners for chess by mail were Canadian or Brazilian. The idea of kissing Westerners was always exciting to Miriam. And Günter, the vegetable lady's husband, whose hobby was model railroading, was constantly writing letters to model-railroad fans in Western Europe. They sent him back model-railroading magazines. Until one day Günter was arrested for spying. The suspicion was beyond absurd. Günter couldn't even stand up to the vegetable lady—why would he want to pick a fight with the state? They threw the book at him anyway, as they always do with sad sacks. When Günter came back, a year and eight months later, he had to use a breathing apparatus that he pulled along behind him on a little wagon.

One day, in the vegetable store, which was no longer a vegetable store, Mrs. Kuppisch saw a man pressing an oxygen mask to his face after taking three steps, to get his breath. Mrs. Kuppisch didn't recognize him until the vegetable lady, who was likewise no longer a vegetable lady, came to the shop door to help him. Everyone who saw Günter gave him half a year, tops, but Günter is still alive and still pulls the little wagon with his oxygen behind him.

The transit cops, finding a registration card for the Dutch course in the sleeve of Mario's ID, promptly reported it on their walkie-talkie. "The individual in custody is enrolled in a Dutch-language course . . . Dutch . . . That's what it says . . . Yes, Dutch."

When a message like that is transmitted, during an ID check at a train station in the border zone, what happens next is automatic. The walkie-talkie responded; two words sufficed. "Arrest him!"

While Mario was waiting to be interrogated, he uncovered a fundamental flaw in the land-purchase math: because two thousand square meters didn't equal two square kilometers, but rather two one-thousandths of a square kilometer, you didn't need to mobilize fifty thousand land buyers, you needed a thousand times that many—fifty million. But the population of the GDR was only seventeen million, and if you subtracted children and comrades you were left with only ten million. Mario had no idea where the missing forty million were supposed to come from. But how, he reassured himself, can they convict me of high treason? Wouldn't it be like convicting a person of attempted murder for being arrested with an unloaded gun?

The interrogator blinded Mario with the desk lamp and said he'd have to earn a glass of water. "You might as well confess everything, we've known all about it for a loooong time! We just want to hear it from you."

Mario assured him that he'd simply fallen asleep on the train. His interrogator laughed at him, roared at him, refused to believe a word he said. Mario stuck to his story. It would have been embarrassing to tell the truth and admit his ridiculous math error. His interrogator could do all the sneering and roaring he wanted. And when Mario, in the middle of the interrogation, actually did fall asleep, it made his story quite credible.

They released him. Never again did he go out land-surveying. The Existentialist knew enough to tell people that Mario proceeded to behave in bed as if he were trying to father the missing forty million land buyers single-handedly.

Micha, too, was once arrested in the border zone. It was the night when the Kuppisches finally got a telephone. They were sitting around the device proudly, feeling as if Christmas had come. And suddenly the thing rang! Mr. Kuppisch cautiously picked up the receiver. But he had to pass it on to Micha, because the call was for him. "A girl," Mr. Kuppisch explained to the curious family.

It was Miriam. Micha was overcome with shyness, and his family didn't show the least consideration.

"Can you make out what she's saying?" Mrs. Kuppisch asked.

"Ask her if she understands what you're saying!" Mr. Kuppisch shouted.

Since everyone was listening, all Micha said was "Mmm," "Yep," "Okay," and "Bye," exactly none of which Miriam understood. She'd expected a bit more when she called Micha. The last time they'd met on the street, Miriam had told him that she wasn't going to be seeing the AWO driver anymore, because he was entering the army for three years. Would Micha be her witness, if the facts were ever in dispute, that her vow hadn't really been a vow, because she'd been crossing her fingers when she said she'd stay faithful to a boyfriend who went in for three years? Micha, after hanging up, ran straight out of the apartment, without a jacket or anything. He called Miriam from the nearest phone booth.

"I'm sorry," he said, panting, "but everyone was listening . . ."

Miriam was reassuring: "It's okay, I just thought you might come over."

But Micha continued to apologize. "See, the reason I couldn't say anything—"

"Sure," Miriam said, "but do you want to come over?"

Micha still didn't get it. "The thing is, we finally got a phone today, and you were the first person who called, so everyone was—"

"So do you want to come over now?" Miriam asked for the third time.

Micha thought he hadn't heard her right. "Sorry—what?"

"I just wanted to know if you might want to come over," Miriam said, angelically patient.

"I'll be right there!" Micha shouted. He hung up the receiver and ran out of the phone booth, straight into the arms of the DPE. "Identification!" Micha was sickened to realize that he'd left his ID in his jacket, and that the jacket was in his apartment. "I'll go get it!" he cried, trying to run, but the DPE wouldn't let go of him. Micha struggled violently to get away, his fists flying, but the DPE was simply stronger. Micha ended up with a bloody nose.

The DPE knew it was all or nothing for Micha that night, but he still bore a grudge against him, because he still hadn't been promoted. It obviously wasn't a question of Micha's name, address, and date of birth, all of which the DPE by now knew better than Micha's mother. Micha was taken to the station on the grounds that "anyone apprehended in the border area without identification documents shall have his personal data verified elsewhere." In the course of the night, the DPE recorded in the logbook that a male individual, not in possession of a valid ID, had been apprehended while running in the border zone and had tried to evade a routine identity check by fleeing. The DPE was just trying to show Micha that he could be nasty, too, but Micha wasn't interested in such subtleties. At this point nothing mattered to him; he hadn't made it to Miriam's, although she'd invited him four times.

The DPE didn't release Micha until the following morning, and now they were even: each of them had thoroughly pissed on the other's parade.

* * *

That day was Micha's first day at the Red Monastery. It was also his last. He got there late, and, as luck would have it, the principal had chosen that moment to give the new students a taste of her joy in enforcement. The new students were crowded in a half circle around the principal, who was glowering at a poster for the Red Monastery chess club. The poster was shaped like a chess king. The student who'd made the poster was summoned, and the principal asked him severely, "What were you thinking?"

The student, who had no idea what he'd done wrong, stammered: "I . . . chess club . . . information . . ."

"Yes, yes," the principal of the Red Monastery interrupted. The new students were all being made witnesses to this scene. "It goes without saying that we have nothing against chess being played at our school, even if the game's inventor didn't believe that a pawn is as valuable as a king, if not more valuable." She paused to give each student time to reflect on this—a pawn, after all, was a worker, while a king was merely a parasite. Then, her expression darkening, she jabbed her index finger at the top of the cardboard king, which flaunted a cross, and cried out in a shrill voice, "But pernicious Christian symbolism will not be tolerated at this school!" At that very moment, as she was grimly pointing to the cross on the king's crown, Micha arrived. He was out of breath and covered in sweat.

"And what's with you?"

Micha was so winded, he could barely answer. "I was . . . arrested . . . in the border zone . . . I tried to get away . . . put up a fight . . ."

"GET OUT!" the principal screamed at him.

Micha had already seen enough. He went back home. His mother burst into tears. She'd done everything she could to get Micha into the Red Monastery and to the Soviet Union for his studies. Mrs. Kuppisch had made sure to put a flag out on every political holiday, she'd quartered youth-festival guests, she'd joined the school parents committee, subscribed to the *ND*, and only used Western plastic bags from Heinz with the writing turned outside in. She'd even called her son Misha. And now, on the very first day, it was over. Mrs. Kuppisch had done everything she could. She cried all day and all night. The next morning, Mr. Kuppisch said: "I'll file a petition!" And then he did something he'd never done before. He actually sat down and wrote a petition.

Two weeks later, Mr. Kuppisch got his reply. He took Micha and Mrs. Kuppisch by the hand and led them, with steely determination, to the Red Monastery. The first thing Micha noticed: the chess poster was now shaped like a pawn.

Mr. Kuppisch barged into the principal's office, paying no attention to the secretary's energetic attempts to stop him. The principal looked up at Mr. Kuppisch with a quizzical frown. Mr. Kuppisch took the letter out of his pocket and read aloud: "Dear Mr. . . . In regard to et cetera, et cetera . . . here!" Finding the part he was looking for, he began to quote from the letter. ". . . we have arranged for the previously imposed relegation to be nullified."

With a triumphant "Hm!" Mr. Kuppisch lowered the letter. "We wrote a petition!" he said with immense satisfaction, and he beckoned Micha and Mrs. Kuppisch into the office, so that the principal could see whom the *we* referred to. Micha didn't come in. Mrs. Kuppisch explained: "Micha had to go. It always happens when he gets excited." This was a lie, but it was the next-to-last lie she would ever tell. Only once more would she portray Micha in an artificial light.

Micha wasn't in the bathroom because he had to go, and he wasn't excited in the least. He'd vanished into the washroom to stand at the mirror and put himself in disarray. When he entered the principal's office, he was chewing gum and the top three buttons of his shirt were brazenly unbuttoned, his hair going every which way. Micha was the picture of a student who would never, ever be tolerated at the Red Monastery. Mrs. Kuppisch immediately started fussing over him, but Micha waved off her intrusions. Mrs. Kuppisch cast a shy glance at the principal, to gauge how devastating an

impression Micha was making but the principal said noth
ing. She merely looked at Micha, and Micha looked at her.
Neither of them had to say anything. Hoping to defuse the
situation, Mrs. Kuppisch attempted one final lie. "Misha,
now that you're at a boarding school, you need to write to
your Soviet pen pal and give him your new address."

Needless to say, Micha didn't have a Soviet pen pal, and
he didn't look like he did. As he and the principal continued
to size each other up, Mr. Kuppisch nervously flapped the letter he'd received in reply to his petition, and encouraged Micha: "Don't just stand there, say something!"

Micha said something he'd once heard Uncle Heinz say,
and then he walked out of the room and left the school. What
he said was enough to ensure that he would never amount to
anything. But at least it freed him from having to be obedient.
Which was exhausting. And Mrs. Kuppisch no longer had to
dream up ways to embellish things. Which was also exhausting. It took her only a few minutes to be perfectly content
with her son's decision. No decent parent, thought Mrs. Kuppisch, would send her children to a school like the Red Monastery. Before long, even Mr. Kuppisch was in good spirits: all
he had to do was think of his petition, and his chest swelled
with pride. "If we'd wanted to, we could have!" he said, waving the letter. "Today we really showed them!"

And so it was that Micha and his parents returned to the
Sonnenallee with their heads held high—even though Micha,
despite years of dogged effort, had failed to land in the Red
Monastery. It had always been so complicated and exhausting, whereas the final stroke was easy. He said, "*Raz, dva,
tri*—Russian we will never be!" and the message was clear.

Life and death on the Sonnenallee

Miriam, for her part, completely ignored Micha in the weeks that followed. She hadn't forgiven him for not coming over, despite being invited four times. Not having heard about Micha's arrest by the DPE, she was immoderately offended by his nonappearance that night: If he won't respond to an invitation like that, what does he want? If he's not responding to me, then who does he want? Micha was irredeemably useless, and Miriam started canoodling with Westerners again. She made no secret of it. Every week, a different car was parked outside her door: first a Porsche, then a Mercedes Cabriolet, then a Jaguar, one time even a Bugatti. The amazing cars that her little brother collected as Matchboxes were now pulling up at Miriam's in real life. Micha was ashen. Every week a different car: he wondered how Miriam did it. But Miriam's little brother told Micha that it wasn't what it looked like. The reality was far worse than Micha had imagined. In exchange for a Big Banger—one of the few cars Miriam had yet to be picked up in—Miriam's little brother produced information: "You think my sister's got a new guy every week. But you're wrong. It's always the same guy. He's just got a different car every week." Even Miriam didn't know how he did it. "The dude must have millions!" Miriam's little brother had an extreme theory: "It's Elvis." But it wasn't Elvis. "But who then? Who is it?" asked Miriam's little brother. Micha, at a loss, said: Maybe he's the Sheik of Berlin.

The Sheik of Berlin did perform one good deed: he opened the huge door of his Cadillac so stupidly that Frizz had no chance of avoiding it with his folding bike. Frizz was thrown to the pavement. If he'd run crying to the DPE, it would have been expensive for the Sheik of Berlin. But Frizz settled it quietly. He needed fifty Western for *Exile on Main Street*. The Sheik of Berlin tried to buy him off with twenty Western, then with fifty Eastern, but Frizz insisted on fifty Western, and eventually he got it. Now Frizz only had to wait for a Tuesday—and then, at long last, he could collect his double album from Edge, who still hung out under the train trestle once a week, selling records.

The Sheik of Berlin had seemed so tightfisted, Frizz began to wonder if he really was the person everyone took him to be. Micha didn't care. Sheik or not, the guy saw Miriam way too often, and he always had way too good a car. And he didn't fit the stereotype. Normally, a man with a conspicuously beautiful car goes through woman after woman, whereas the Sheik of Berlin, a man with a conspicuously beautiful *woman*, went through car after car. There was no competing with a man who was constantly showing up, each time with a new car. Micha's nerves were raw. One day, after again being laughed at by a school group on the platform on the West Berlin side, he shouted back in a rage: "As soon as I'm eighteen, I'm going to be stationed at the border for three years—and then I'm going to shoot down every one of you!" No one on the Sonnenallee had ever seen Micha so enraged. But his outburst did have one benefit: he was never laughed at again.

The Sheik of Berlin was, in reality, the parking-lot attendant at the Hotel Schweizerhof. He knew which guests would leave their cars in the garage for the duration of their stay at the hotel. The Sheik of Berlin helped himself to their cars. It was an ideal method of seeming filthy rich. But then one day things went awry. It wasn't a fender bender. It wasn't a serious accident. It was even worse. Far worse than anything the Sheik of Berlin could have imagined. He was coming over in a Lamborghini, and there were difficulties at the checkpoint: in the trunk of the car were four submachine guns. The Sheik of Berlin had borrowed the Lamborghini without realizing that it belonged to the Mafia. Submachine guns being submachine guns, the Sheik of Berlin was interrogated by the Stasi for several days. Then they let him go. Neither the Lamborghini nor the guns were returned to him. The Mafiosi were waiting for him at the border crossing. It was exactly as he'd feared: there they stood, three Sicilians staring holes in the air, idly buffing their nails. The Sheik of Berlin had put his troubles with the Stasi behind him, but now he saw that his *real* troubles were ahead of him. He returned to the checkpoint and politely asked if he might be allowed to become a citizen of the GDR. The guards sent him away. The Sicilians were still standing on the opposite street corner. The Sheik of Berlin turned around and pleaded with the guards to make him a citizen of the GDR. Again he was refused. The third time, he came back crying and fell to his knees, begging to be made a citizen of the GDR. A guard picked up the phone and spoke with the ministry. There they took pity on him. The Sheik of Berlin became a citizen of the GDR and a pedestrian. But that was the end of him and Miriam. If he was living with a target on his back, she said, there was no such thing as too much distance between them.

* * *

The remarkable thing about the Wall was that the people who lived there didn't find the Wall the least bit extraordinary. It was so much a part of their daily life, they hardly noticed it, and if the Wall had secretly been opened up they would have been the last to notice.

But then something did happen that reminded the people at the short end of the Sonnenallee of where they lived, and it happened in the way that everyone had always hoped it never would. Afterward, everyone tried to find out what had occurred that night, and how it could possibly have occurred.

Micha had often unwillingly witnessed Miriam's smooching with the Sheik of Berlin. In his impotence, he returned to pursuing his idiotic old plan to lay hands on her love letter, which was still in the death strip. His thoughts were so entirely focused on the letter, it assumed the dimensions of a mental illness. Micha had the crazy idea of enlisting for army service at the border and then reading the letter from the nearest watchtower, using an optical device constructed out of binoculars and a rifle scope. He immersed himself so deeply in optical formulas, and acquired such technical mastery of concepts like focal length, refraction, and axial backscatter coefficients, he was able to do the necessary calculations by himself.

Sometimes he also just stood by the part of the Wall that the letter was on the other side of. Like a dog at his master's grave, howling at the moon. One Tuesday night, when the moon actually did happen to be full, Frizz ran into him there.

"Hello, Micha!" Frizz called out, in high spirits. "What are you doing here?"

Micha didn't understand how Frizz could be in such a good mood. How anyone could be in a good mood in a world in which a love letter from the most beautiful girl, the absolutely most beautiful, goes missing. Micha proceeded to pour out his heart to Frizz. "Her letter's over there, you understand, her letter is right behind this wall, and I can't get to it!"

Frizz was surprised. "And why can't you?"

"Why *not*?" Micha said. "It's the death strip, man, you'll get shot if you go in there."

Frizz looked at Micha as if he didn't understand what the problem was. "I'll tell you tomorrow," he said. He was in a rush to leave, but Micha wouldn't let him. Frizz apparently knew the answer to Micha's most important question!

"How would it work?" Micha wanted to know.

"The questions you ask." Frizz shook his head and rolled his eyes. Then he pointed at Micha's building. "That's your apartment, right?"

"As if I didn't know that!" Micha had no idea where Frizz was going with this.

"Well, so, if you had an extension cord, you could plug your vacuum cleaner in here."

"Yeah? And what am I supposed to do with a *vacuum cleaner*?"

Frizz pointed to a pile of construction debris that had been in front of Micha's building for years. In the middle of the pile was a long remnant of flexible tubing. "All you have to do is stick one end of the tube in the vacuum cleaner and put the other end in the death strip."

Micha was speechless—the idea was pure genius. He just had to keep raking around with the hose in the vicinity of the letter. Sooner or later, the letter would get sucked onto the end of the tube. Micha ran and got a vacuum cleaner and a long coil of power cord from his apartment. Frizz had no choice but to help him, although he didn't want to.

* * *

Everyone was a little more amped up than usual that night, perhaps because the moon was full. The Existentialist, roaming the city with Mario, was ranting in a way she hadn't in a long time. "Man, I'm telling you, I've had enough of this shit. You know? It's like, I'm a painter, but what's there to paint here? You only need one color—gray. You've only got one look on your face, and that's being sick of it. Man, you know, I got some paints from a friend over there, these paints that everybody here's so keen on, because the colors are so bright or whatever. And you know something? I couldn't do a fucking thing with them. What are you supposed to paint with bright colors? Man, it's like they're even clamping down on color. When it gets to the point where even the flags are too red for them, I'm telling you, they mean business! No wonder everybody's getting out of here. The people who haven't already taken off all want to take off. And the people who don't want to take off will figure it out soon enough. And the last person out can turn off the lights."

At that very moment, as if by some miracle, the lights all around them really did go out. Mario and the Existentialist were left standing in the dark. It was just an ordinary power outage, but it came exactly on cue and it happened in the border zone. This was unprecedented—a power outage in the border zone. It was so weird, the Existentialist burst into sobs and threw her arms around Mario's neck.

"Shit, Mario. Now we really are the last ones. They forgot about us. Please don't leave me alone. Me and—the baby."

Mario thought he'd misheard. "The baby?" he asked. She nodded. This was how Mario learned that he was going to be a father.

* * *

The power failed at precisely the moment when the border guard plugged the complicated Japanese stereo system into the East German power grid. There was a flicker—and out went the lights in the death strip and all the neighboring residential streets. The darkness was total. Being well-versed in conspiracy theories, the guard instantly understood that the Japanese stereo system was a kind of Trojan horse; that it had been cleverly placed in the hands of the customs officials with the single, solitary objective of causing a power failure.

And so the guard set off the general alarm. With a cry of "Border alarm!" he fired a flare gun into the sky, up toward the full moon, which might have been the reason why everyone was so amped up that night.

When the first flare was shot into the sky, Mr. and Mrs. Kuppisch went up to the roof, the better to follow the spectacle. They put their arms around each other and cried "Oh!" and "Ah!" The fireworks were like nothing they'd ever seen, either on New Year's Eve or the Republic's anniversary day or for any kind of youth festival.

Micha and Frizz, of course, were also affected by the power outage. The vacuum cleaner died before the two of them had gotten hold of the letter with their contraption. They were in the process of retracting the long hose when they were spotted by the border soldiers. The burning magnesium of the flares emitted a glaring light, casting multiple hard shadows against the Wall. The rise and fall of the flares animated and contorted the shadows of Micha and Frizz and their mysterious apparatus. Their hectic movements made them look like terrorists: the shadows collided or drifted away from each other, lurching in every direction, billowing up and then suddenly vanishing. It would never have occurred to a border guard that the two of them were simply trying to get a love letter out of the death strip with a vacuum cleaner and a very long hose. In the spooky play of light and shadow from the flares, it was utterly impossible to look harmless. Not to mention the full moon.

When the shot was fired, everyone on the Sonnenallee knew it wasn't a shot from a flare gun, and when Frizz lay motionless on the pavement everyone knew the shot had found its mark. Micha was still with him, and he was quickly joined by Mario and the Existentialist. Mr. and Mrs. Kuppisch hurried down from the roof to see what had happened, likewise the DPE, who had his responsibilities. Soon Miriam and her little brother were there as well. Frizz lay in the street, not stirring, and everyone was wailing. The bullet had ripped through his jacket by his heart. It was what everyone had always hoped they would never see. But now it had happened. Frizz moved a little. The Existentialist kneeled down to at least get him comfortably settled while he died—but suddenly Frizz sat up. He unbuttoned his jacket and, still in a daze, pulled out *Exile on Main Street*. The record was shot to pieces, but it had saved his life.

Frizz began to cry. "A genuine English pressing!" he sobbed, pulling the shards of *Exile* from its tattered sleeve. "It was new! And sealed! And now *both* of them are ruined! It was a double album!" Frizz was nothing but a mess of tears.

"Frizz," said the Existentialist, "if there'd only been one of them . . ." She didn't dare complete the thought.

"One wouldn't have been enough, Frizz," Mr. Kuppisch said.

"Okay, okay," Frizz said, racked with sobs. "But still!"

And then Micha saw the love letter fly out of the death strip and over the Wall. The letter was burning brightly. A descending flare had landed on the letter and ignited it, and the letter, carried aloft by its own heat, flew back to the short side of the Sonnenallee, an ash of itself. Micha watched the burning letter, and after it had burned itself out he looked at

Miriam. All at once, Miriam understood what had happened. Not every detail, of course, but it was clear to her that, somehow or other, the shooting had had to do with her.

A few days later, Miriam and Micha ran into each other on the street. It was one of the last warm days of the year. Miriam was wearing her summer dress one more time, with nothing underneath. Micha was unwrapping an ice cream on a stick. As Miriam poured out her heart to him, Micha didn't dare lick his ice cream; he probably found it *uncool*, although the word didn't exist in German back then. The ice cream dripped onto his hand and ran down his forearm.

Both of them had a guilty conscience: Miriam had underestimated how deeply Micha had suffered on her account, and Micha had taken his love-letter mania too far. If Frizz hadn't been so indescribably lucky, Micha wouldn't have wanted to go on living. At the very least, a shadow would have fallen on his life forever. Would have; might have; could have . . .

Miriam raised the subject of her smooching fixation. She was sorry that Micha had been so hurt by her making out with Westerners. She tried to explain to Micha that *they* wanted to regulate everything, *they* prohibited everything. By *they*, of course, she didn't mean Westerners but everyone from Erdmute Löffeling on up. The people who called the shots. "They want to forbid everything, deny us everything," Miriam said. And she needed some way to defend herself, she needed some way to feel that not everything was forbidden to her. Making out with Westerners gave her the feeling that *they* didn't have total control of her, because . . .

While she was searching for a word, Micha became aware that his ice cream was about to fall off its stick. Simply to cut things short, he interrupted Miriam. Did she maybe want to go to the movies? *Around the World in 80 Days* was playing. Miriam, who was trying to find words for her longing, her horror of constriction, her yearning for foreign places, felt as if she'd been delivered. "Finally, someone who understands me!" Micha understood nothing at all, but as Miriam was leaving, freed of her oppression, he gave her a wave—and what was left of his ice cream sailed onto the front of his shirt.

At the cinema, they saw the travels of Phileas Fogg and his servant, Passepartout, they saw Moors and belly dancers, jungles and deserts, hot-air balloons and steamboats, crocodiles, buffaloes, and elephants carrying palanquins. Micha had reverted to his shyness and didn't dare put his arm around Miriam, even though the movie was overlong and Miriam was snuggling against his shoulder.

When they emerged from the theater, tanks were rolling down the Karl-Marx-Allee. It was just a drill for the military parade on the Seventh of October, but the two of them were back to knowing exactly where they were. The tanks were loud and stinking, and it was hard to imagine a starker contrast to the light and the colors of the movie. Miriam, in tears, threw herself into Micha's arms, and Micha hugged her and held her tightly, trying to console her. But there was no consoling her: the movie had made her *soft*, and then suddenly the tanks in the night—Miriam simply wasn't made for such a brutal juxtaposition.

The whole way back, she was doggedly silent; at most, she might have shaken her head. When she got home, she went to bed without speaking to anyone. In the morning, she stayed in bed and just stared at the ceiling. She responded to nothing and to no one. The next day, too, and the day after that, she lay in bed despondently. She took some tea, a bit of soup. Her family was understandably worried. They didn't know what was wrong with her. They were also reluctant to say anything to Micha, knowing how sensitive he was, how quick he was to blame himself for everything. It fell to the DPE to tell Micha to go and see Miriam. "Your girl isn't doing too well."

As Micha sat with Miriam by her bed, he became deeply unsettled. He'd heard stories of people falling apart in this country, and he had only one wish: to save Miriam. He'd always wanted to save her. He used to wish that a fire would break out, even a war, so that he could save her from it—and now he sensed that someone needed to come and save her. And he wanted to be this someone. He leaned over her and said, "You know, I often feel the way you're feeling, and I always write about it in my diary. You're not alone, though, you really aren't. You're not alone." Miriam gave no sign of response, either then or when Micha promised her: "I'll read them to you tomorrow, my diaries." He said goodbye and dashed back to his apartment, hung a DO NOT ENTER sign on his door, and got to work. The problem was that Micha had never kept a diary. And now he had to.

The first diary was the hardest, because Micha had to write it with his left hand, so the handwriting would look unpracticed. He reckoned that the longer he'd kept a diary, the greater its effect on Miriam would be. All through the night, Micha sat up with his diaries and reflected on what it meant to live here at the short end of the Sonnenallee, where things just went the way they went. And he wrote that he'd always loved her, because he felt that she was something special, and that there was something alive in her that went beyond her, and that she always gave him hope and he wished her success in everything, everything, everything. He knew he would be reading all these confessions aloud to her, but it made no difference to him. To cheer Miriam up, to save her, he was prepared to do anything. Anything.

The next morning, Mrs. Kuppisch found Micha asleep over his final diary. Micha's head was lying on the open diary, his hands grubby with ink, and on his desk were seven empty ink cartridges. Yes, seven! Genghis Khan sired seven children in one night, but Micha had emptied seven ink cartridges in one night.

* * *

When Micha went to Miriam with his diaries, she was lying in bed with the same lifeless expression she'd worn for days, her eyes fixed on the ceiling. Micha opened the first diary and showed it to her. "Here, see," he said, "it started out more like a scrawl than writing." Miriam didn't respond in the slightest. "Okay, then," Micha said, clearing his throat, "I'm going to read it to you. 'Dear Diary! Today was an important day, because we finally learned how to write capital letters. Now it's worth starting a diary, because I can finally write a very important word the way I used to be able to only think it: S-H-I-T!'"

Miriam smiled. Not wanting to be interrupted when he'd barely started, Micha raised a hand: "Wait, wait, it goes on from there—" But he stopped short, seeing that Miriam had returned to life. She was taking things in again—she was listening, reacting, smiling! Micha was overjoyed: "Did you . . . Did I . . ." Miriam smiled, she beamed, and by and by she threw her arms around his neck, pulling him down to her, and finally made good on her promise: she showed him how Westerners kiss.

Miriam's little brother stood watching in the doorway. It's about time, he thought.

Then he went down to the grounds, made a deal for a Matchbox Stretcha Fetcha, and told Mario and the Existentialist, Frizz, Fatty, Lensy, and Shrapnel how Miriam had been saved by Micha. "People, that is love!" said Miriam's little brother, and they all nodded thoughtfully, saying nothing. And as the shadow of a cloud flew over them, they shivered.

* * *

That afternoon, when Micha left Miriam and went home, elated, Mrs. Kuppisch opened the door for him in tears. "Heinz is . . . dead!" she said, pointing to the living room. Heinz was sitting in the armchair, dead. "Lung cancer!" said Sabine, who was also in tears. "The doctor thinks it was lung cancer."

The doorbell rang, and Mr. Kuppisch opened the door. Standing outside it, offering his condolences to the Kuppisch family, was the Stasi neighbor. He even wore a black suit. "I have always maintained discretion with regard to my professional activities," he said, somewhat awkwardly. "But since we've been neighbors for so long . . ." He beckoned to a pair of men in the hallway, who proceeded to maneuver a coffin into the cramped apartment. This was how the Kuppisches learned that their neighbor was a mortician. Mr. Kuppisch was so surprised, the color drained from his face. His neighbor poured him a schnapps. "Come now, Mr. Kuppisch, it's not unusual that your circulation should fail you. But this is, after all, our daily bread." Mr. Kuppisch threw back the schnapps, and then, feeling better, blurted out to his neighbor the first thought that came to mind: "Better a mortician neighbor than a Stasi neighbor. Now at least we know where we stand." The neighbor had no idea what might have moved Mr. Kuppisch to make this comparison, but he nodded as if he understood. And then he got to work.

The mere sight of the coffin being opened made Micha's heart clutch. Mrs. Kuppisch's eyes were so full of tears, she no longer even recognized her dead brother. Bernd asked Sabine where her servant of God was, for extreme unction and Heaven and so forth, but Sabine sobbed and said, "It was too boring with him . . . I mean, a vow of chastity, Papa, have you ever heard of such a thing?" And when Heinz was being placed in the coffin, a thing happened that brought tears to Micha's own eyes: a roll of Smarties fell from Heinz's pants leg.

Heinz could have been the greatest of smugglers, Micha thought. At least once, though, he would have had to bring over something illegal, a bomb, or "Moscow," or porno magazines . . . "Anything but stuff like this!" Micha sobbed as he picked up the Smarties.

Mrs. Kuppisch received permission to cross the border for Heinz's funeral. It was the first time anyone from the short end of the Sonnenallee had been allowed to travel to the West. Maybe she was allowed to go because she was leaving her family behind as collateral. Or because she'd always put the flag out, had subscribed to the *ND*, had offered quarters for youth-festival guests . . . Mrs. Kuppisch was allowed to spend only one night in the West. On her return, she placed a can of coffee on the table. "Did I ever smuggle!"

"Not this again," Micha groaned. "Mama, coffee is totally legal, you don't have to smuggle it, you'd have been better off . . ."

Mr. Kuppisch, curious, had already opened the can and raised it to his nose to savor it. "This isn't any coffee!"

Bernd reached into the can. Fine black crumbs caked on his fingertips. "This looks more like . . ." He frowned, rubbing the powder between his fingers. It wasn't drugs.

Sabine was the first to guess. "Hey, is that Uncle Heinz?" Mrs. Kuppisch nodded proudly.

For a minute, Micha, Sabine and Bernd, and Mr. and Mrs. Kuppisch silently contemplated the contents of the can. "Peace be on his ashes," Mr. Kuppisch said finally, putting the lid back on the can. No one would have guessed that they would witness yet another of Heinz's exciting coups of smuggling. But this one topped everything: Heinz himself had been smuggled over the border. There couldn't have been a more fitting end.

In the evening, Heinz was laid to rest beneath a chestnut tree in the cemetery on Baumschulenweg. The phrase *quiet funeral* had never been more apt, even though the people from the short end of the Sonnenallee had come out in force, including the DPE and the border guard. The eulogy was very short. "Heinz," Mr. Kuppisch said solemnly, "you were

more than just our brother-in-law, our brother, our uncle—
you were our Western relative!"

They scattered dirt on the grave and then they all went
home, talking among themselves along the way. Micha was
the only one who didn't join the conversations. He was thinking about what he should do with his diaries. He'd read only
the very first day of his entries to Miriam; the best was still
to come. Am I going to be a writer? he asked himself. Nah,
he thought. How could I ever describe it without a reader
shaking his head? I only have to hear the *importance* they
attach to whatever they're talking about. The Existentialist
was telling Mario about a new book on child-rearing that had
appeared in the West, and how, when their child was born,
she wanted to raise it like a Ye'kuana Indian. The DPE was
vouchsafing that he would definitely get his promotion at the
next Anniversary Day. Frizz was reporting that Centrum had
been selling licensed editions of Western records last Friday.
Mr. Kuppisch was repeating, for the fifth time, that it was a
lucky thing they'd voted, because no way would Mrs. Kuppisch have been allowed to cross the border if they hadn't.
And he wondered what it meant that the Alschers, who lived
on the third floor, had control of the building's books—they
were guaranteed to be Stasi . . .

Man, the air we moved, Micha wrote later. *It would have
gone on like that forever. It made you sick from top to bottom,
but we had such splendid fun. We were so smart, so well-read,
so interested, but it all added up to something idiotic. Even as we
charged into the future, we were stuck in some kind of yesterday.
My God, we were funny, and we didn't even know it.*

It would have gone on like that forever, except that something intervened.

* * *

Mario and the Existentialist had bought an old Trabi, but Mario wasn't allowed to drive it until he turned eighteen, and even then he would have to go to driving school, which wouldn't be so easy, because his hair was long again. But then, to make money, Mario decided to become an illegal taxi driver. There were hardly any taxis, none at all when you needed one, and anyone who owned a car and needed money worked illegally as a taxi driver. And he needed money soon, because the Existentialist was already eight months along.

Mario occupied himself with the car day and night. Nothing about the old Trabant worked; literally everything had to be repaired. Ever since they bought the car, the Existentialist had seen nothing of Mario but his feet. "How does such a simple car break down so often!" she cried out one day. While Mario was assuring her, "No, it's just sometimes the cap nut on the coupling sleeve gets caught on the drive pinion . . ." she felt her first contraction.

"Oh God, Mario, it's starting!" the Existentialist screamed. Mario crawled out from under the car. "Get on the phone!" she screamed. "Call a taxi!"

"We don't *have* phones here! We don't *have* taxis! I'll drive you!"

"With what?" the Existentialist said desperately. Then it dawned on her what Mario had in mind. "Mario, we've had this thing for six weeks and you haven't driven it three feet!"

"Then it's time to try!" Mario turned the ignition key, and, lo and behold, the motor started. "That simply isn't possible," Mario murmured. He helped the Existentialist into the passenger seat, shut the door, and roared out of the entryway where he'd been working on the car. Rain was pouring from the sky. As the car shot into the street, he lost the exhaust pipe on the curb, the muffler along with it. The car rattled atrociously. The Existentialist was afraid that their baby would be permanently damaged. Being born in a Trabi was as bad as entering the world in the middle of an air raid. And Mario wasn't very considerate. He shouted gleefully, over the noise, "Even the wipers are working, did you see that?" Details like these didn't interest the Existentialist. She only wanted to escape the rattling inferno before her child arrived.

But then suddenly the drive seemed to be over. A traffic cop was blocking the street.

"Let us through!" Mario shouted. "We're having a baby!"

"Turn off your engine," the officer said. "We need to let the Soviet delegation through."

"No," Mario shouted, "we're having the baby right now!" He put the car in gear again and shot back onto the arterial. As he later told his friends at the grounds, "When your girlfriend's in labor, a state visit is meaningless."

Mario was turning onto the main road when the delegation passed him: thirteen state vehicles barreling into town at top speed. But Mario was faster. He quickly caught up with the rearmost car and then, one by one, began to pass the others. The Existentialist was lying on the passenger seat, drenched in sweat, already well into labor. Mario had passed nearly the entire motorcade when a pair of cars veered out and caught him in a pincer movement, forcing him to stop. Mario's engine stalled. He tried to restart it, without success. He climbed out and stood in the pouring rain. The Existentialist was keening and gasping. Mario had never felt more helpless, and all he could think to do, in his desperation, was to make entreating and imploring gestures in the direction of the dark-windowed state vehicles. Sure enough, a car door opened, and one of the Russians got out. He had a large birthmark on his forehead, which gave him a scary appearance at first glance. "Please," Mario said bravely. "We're having a baby!" The Russian made a simple hand gesture at the sky—and instantly the rain stopped. Then he leaned into the car, where the Existentialist was in labor. She was groaning and screaming. The Russian fiddled around in the passenger compartment for a few moments, and then he emerged from the car holding a neatly swaddled newborn, which he placed in Mario's arms. His two hands now free, the Russian touched the hood of the Trabi. The car started right up again.

"That is a Russian who works miracles!" the Existentialist shouted. "Ask him what his name is."

Mario nervously asked him: "*Kak tebja sawut?*" But the miracle-working Russian had already gotten back in his car, with a laugh, and driven away.

Mario and Elisabeth stood in the street with their baby, watching the state vehicles go by, and the farther the motorcade receded into the distance, the clearer it became to the two of them that a thing had just happened to them that no one would believe. And their child, too, would become larger, would grow and learn to ask questions, would listen . . . But the things in this country would probably be as incomprehensible to the child as they were to its parents.

If you truly want to preserve what's happened, you can't indulge in memories. Human memory is far too comforting a process to simply capture the past; it's the opposite of what it pretends to be. For memory is capable of more, much more: it stubbornly performs the miracle of making peace with the past, wherein every old grudge evaporates and the soft veil of nostalgia settles over all the things that once felt sharp and lacerating.

Happy people have bad memory but rich memories.